Don't Tell Me What to Do

DINA DEL BUCCHIA

 Arsenal Pulp Press
Vancouver

ARSENAL PULP PRESS
Suite 202 – 211 East Georgia St.
Vancouver, BC V6A 1Z6
Canada
arsenalpulp.com

The publisher gratefully acknowledges the support of the Canada Council for the Arts and the British Columbia Arts Council for its publishing program, and the Government of Canada, and the Government of British Columbia (through the Book Publishing Tax Credit Program), for its publishing activities.

BRITISH COLUMBIA | BRITISH COLUMBIA ARTS COUNCIL *An agency of the Province of British Columbia* | Canada Council for the Arts   Conseil des arts du Canada | Canadä

This is a work of fiction. Any resemblance of characters to persons either living or deceased is purely coincidental.

Cover and text design by Oliver McPartlin
Edited by Robyn So

Printed and bound in Canada

Library and Archives Canada Cataloguing in Publication:
Del Bucchia, Dina, 1979-
[Short stories. Selections]
    Don't tell me what to do / Dina Del Bucchia.

 Short stories.
Issued in print and electronic formats.
ISBN 978-1-55152-701-7 (softcover).--ISBN 978-1-55152-702-4
(HTML)

    I. Title. II. Title: Do not tell me what to do.

PS8607.E482538A6 2017   C813'.6   C2017-904059-6
                                             C2017-904060-X

Contents

Keeping Things Alive Is Too Much Work

"We call them blades, but they can't cut nothing," Ron says, chuckling at what he thinks is a joke.

Val rakes a swath of yellow grass into another pile; the scratch of the rake blocks out her neighbour's voice. Mounds of shorn grass dot her wide yard, rustle in the wind. They almost pulse as if under their scruff lies a mulchy beating heart.

"Okay, Ron. Whatever you say." She wipes a gardening glove across her sweaty forehead. It's too early for Ron's nonsense and for it to be so hot, but the right time of day to get work done.

Ron has been watching her since she came out this morning. Not sure what was so interesting about her pushing the mower around in neat lines, about the way she rakes, slower than she used to. And he doesn't seem to be going anywhere as she admires her grassy hills before loading them into the wheelbarrow and carting them to the alley. And he's still there to see her uncoil the hose and spray down the dusty flowerbeds, turn on the sprinkler.

"Not looking too good there. Everything looks near dead if you ask me."

Val didn't ask him and what does she care what he or anyone else thinks. She goes inside, slams the sliding glass door. He better not set up camp outside her front window and watch her watch people root around in other people's storage lockers on television.

She makes herself more coffee, puts bread in the toaster. A splash of water hits the kitchen window. The placement of the sprinkler is slightly off. The house doesn't need watering.

Her granddaughter, Rae, is always talking about the environment, how we're wasting everything away.

"Resources," she says. "Water. Every time you turn on the faucet the world dies a little. It doesn't just come flowing out of the tap from nowhere."

Val knows water flowing out of a tap isn't magic. Just because she didn't go to college, dropped out of high school to get married to someone with a decent wage, doesn't mean she's confused about the world. She dumped her husband fifteen years ago. Doesn't need a GED to know it's the smartest move she ever made. Her days are her own. Her life her own because someone doesn't think they own her.

Rae comes by for bottle drives, bikes over with energy-efficient light bulbs, a special box to collect batteries, checks up on people's recycling, and sets up robot-like composters around the neighbourhood. Each one decorated by local artists, painted with vegetable-based paints. At night the composters look like intruders, something from space ready to abduct humans, crumple their bodies into manure. She spends weekends raising money for clean water in far-away countries by selling organic, gluten-free pastries.

Val's grandson, Justin, is always talking about snowboards. So he's into water too. Frozen water crystals all packed up on a mountain.

"It's best in the powder, Gramma. The board moves so sick."

"I'd be sick if I was swooshing around on a board down a steep hill."

"Are you going to tell me you had to walk to school up a mountain in your day?"

"Nope. I know things are different."

The environment and snowboarding. Both endeavours seem equally taxing to Val. This weekend when they come for lunch, she'll be prepared to talk about it all. She can look up anything on her tablet.

"Hi, Mom. Your yard looks so sad." Her son, Ben, hugs her. Insults always pair best with hugs.

"Yard doesn't have feelings."

"Nice one, Gramma," says her grandson.

"But—" Ben tries to get a word in.

"But, it's smack dab in the middle of summer, and I do my best without a tree for shade out there. Can only water on odd days. Yard's just balding, like you."

He stands at the back window, children on either side of him. The three of them looking out at the dusty brown scraps of grass, shrivelled weeds, bare patches that sprout more evenly than the lawn itself.

"Do you like that? Is it better than television? Staring at an old woman's failure. Just paint a picture and put it up in your own damn living room. Then you can look at it every day, like some kind of art. Okay, that's enough."

She ushers them into the kitchen, huffs until they're all seated at the table, and pours juice from a plastic jug into their glasses.

Rae says, "I told you to get rid of your plastics that aren't BPA free. I don't want you to get cancer." She examines the pitcher, rotates it in front of her. "There must be some way to re-use this."

Crisp salad sits in the middle of the table in a metal bowl.

"I've got green things for you right here."

Val points. She brings in chips and a pyramid of triangular sandwiches. Everyone takes a sandwich. No one mentions how unhealthy chips are as they heap handfuls on their plates until there isn't much room left for salad.

Ten years ago, when the teenagers were kids, Val's son took her with them on a family vacation to the Grand Coulee Dam. It seemed like everything had to be educational, even a weekend getaway. Val packed a cooler with triangular sandwiches and chips in Ziploc bags.

They all stood on the viewing deck. The cascades of water

looked so beautiful. Photos were taken of all of them standing surrounded by the rich blue water, the crisp blue sky, and the slate grey of the massive structure.

Inside they walked past photographs of construction, the before and after. Rae asked why things were less green, then more green? Justin stared at the rushing water through the window, an almost dangerous level of interest. Val kept coming back to the massive images of the dry dam. When the valves were shut it was so smooth. Concrete slopes looked simple and pristine. Flat lines, cold contours. It was more beautiful that way. Clean. Constructed to harness nature.

When the water burst through, everything became animated, chaotic. Even though it was controlled, the gushing sound was overwhelming. There was a laser light show too. Educational and electric. It was everything the river was not: flashy and colourful, an attempt to take the flow into man's hands.

Val had wished they'd been photographed in front of the grey, empty, curved flumes. So peaceful.

"Time for dessert. It's pie and ice cream. And, yes, I got organic blueberries, dammit."

Val half-heartedly drags the sprinkler a few feet from where it's spraying up against the house on one side and the shed on the other. Water tings and spatters against glass and metal. Droplets dribble down the outside of the window. She likes the sound. She likes the look of it. Streaks blur her view of the inside of her home.

"You're a drip, Val."

Ron's sipping on a Mike's Hard Lemonade through a straw. He's in his same spot, camped out with a beverage on his weathered lawn chair. If it wasn't empty on occasion, it could be said that Ron's moulded to the fabric seat. If he didn't move his hand to his mouth, his arm might be glued to the rest. Beside him is what looks like a new cooler. Blue plastic, white lid, not too big. Easily fits a six-pack, and maybe a box of popsicles. He's always in the chair or not. Just appears and disappears.

"Yeah, you're working real hard over there. You're gonna break your wrist if you're not careful."

"You know I'm only teasing." Ron holds out his Mike's Hard to Val, winks at her.

"Do I?"

There's barely a need to cut the grass anymore. The only yard work is this half-assed watering, a vain attempt to keep some of the lawn alive. It's not working. Everything's brown. Even the clover that didn't succumb to the sugar and water, the corn gluten meal, the chemical poisons. She'd fed that clover perfectly good sugar and perfectly good poison. She'd wanted to kill that clover, and now it was dead. Because everything was dead. And now everyone was on her case about how terrible it looked. They'd been on her case about how terrible the clover had looked too. Ron told her that clover was a sign of low nitrogen or something. Her son gave her lawn a solemn look, gave her the downturned eyebrows of pity.

"It's real hot out, Val." Ron drains the yellow sugary alcohol like a kid drinking a pop.

"Oh, really?" Val's hands are still gripped tight to the hose. She might as well just shut the whole thing down. Give up. Go inside. Or head to the store and stock up on her own supply of cold alcoholic beverages. Nothing so sweet though. Just regular old beer.

"C'mon, now. Won't hurt you to wet your throat. Or any other parts."

"I'm not in the mood for that talk. Ever."

"Be fun. Come on and have a drink." Ron opens his cooler, jammed as tight as can be with pastel pink and yellow bottled drinks.

Val yanks the hose toward herself, stands in the spray. Behind her Ron's caught in the shower too. He drops one drink, gets up, and runs inside. The first time she's seen him move in years.

Each night it gets worse. Val can't sleep. Her house heats up like a brick oven, and even with three fans pointed at her she can't cool down. The blades chop the air. Val imagines each cutting through this thick heat, this stench. She wills each swipe to help her ease into sleep, tries to count the rotations like sheep to help herself stay in control. She lolls for a few minutes at a time, falling into strange dreams. None of it feels like sleep.

She's standing on a knife-edge, and it's dangerous but cool. Her ex-husband is chastising her from their old Winnebago, that she's ruined their house, let it go to rot, but he won't just drive away. She wakes up in a wheelbarrow full of crispy grass, but really wakes up in bed.

In some gardening magazine her son gave her a subscription to, a subscription she didn't want or care about, she remembers reading that lawns were originally for rich people. Poor people were throwing their shit out their windows into the street, onto other people. They didn't have a patch of green to try not to kill. Rich people had servants to fluff up their shrubs.

Everyone wants to pretend to be rich. That's where lawns came from. Everyone thinking they're better than everyone else. Everyone wanting to pretend they're the aristocracy and not peasants working just to make their life not a terrible, shitty mess.

How the hell did her son get the idea that she wanted a gardening magazine? What did she do that made anyone think she cared about gardening? Just get old? Did she look useless? It's supposed to be contemplative, he'd said. Val was thinking about shit all the damn time. She had plenty of time to think, being a retired woman with a paid-off mortgage.

The clock says four a.m. It's the coolest part of the night. She might sleep until six-thirty a.m. Could plan her day around a nap that'll barely register.

What would happen if people looked into her yard and didn't see green grass? What would happen if she just tilled the whole thing up? If she decided to let it die? What else could live out there so simply? Who decided to put grass out there any-way? Her house isn't Versailles. She Googles it all. Makes a list of supplies she'll need to transform her lawn from the living dead into something else.

"It's dead anyway," she says into the sticky air, the whir of fan blades, herself.

"It's dead anyway," she says to her son at their next Sunday family lunch.

He'd suggested they eat outside. Val reminded him that there's no table, no chairs, no umbrella, no fans to stave off heat. He said that's okay. They can spread a blanket, have a picnic. Rae thought it a nice idea. Val said a flat out no. End of discussion. Justin was out with friends, skateboarding for a birthday or something.

Val opens the curtains so they can look outside, see the backyard in all its faded glory. "I miss the voles."

"Grandma, they were so cute. Me, too, I hated when Grandpa tried to poison them."

The voles were cute, like the small mice found at pet stores for snake feed.

"I can't believe you remember that, Rae. You were barely two years old."

Those voles used to annoy the shit out of her husband. Oh, he tried to murder them, tried to flush them out with the hose once. He tried everything, but nothing worked. Those voles outsmarted and outlasted him. And yet, somehow, once he left they never came back, moved on to greener lawns, she supposed. Wanting the voles back to ruin her lawn is funny, since she's already ruined it herself. A sad lawn isn't a happy home for any self-respecting vole.

She baked Ben's favourite cookies in the middle of the night, and a lemon pie. Insomnia baking. It made her feel useful. Hopes it's useful now. Slicing pie, she gives him the fattest slice.

"Can I borrow your truck?"

"Sure. For what?"

Explaining to her son why she needs to borrow his truck is more annoying that she'd realized it would be. She doesn't need a lawn. She's got a plan. To get rid of the lawn. To tear it up, to smooth it out. Fill the space with perfect unmowable concrete, concrete that won't burn in August heat. Concrete that will shine in the daylight. That she can sweep away dirt from. That she can admire in any season.

"That's not very environmentally sound, Grandma."

"Wasting water isn't good for the environment. And that's all I'm doing out there, Rae."

"That's a big job, Mom."

"Don't need it. Who goes back there anyway? Nobody sees it except for that creep, Ron."

No one does go back there. She was never one for hosting parties, hadn't invited anyone into her yard in years and years. It's all work and no play.

"We could have barbecues. You could start a book club back there."

"Can pretend to talk about books and drink wine inside just fine. Just let me know what days I can have the truck. I won't scratch it. It's a very nice truck. This is what I'm doing.

Keeping things alive is too much work."

She packs the cookies into a plastic container for him to take home.

"You kept me alive."

"Yeah, and your sister. And she barely talks to me. Two people is enough to keep alive for one lifetime."

It's so hot that she dreams her whole yard is on fire. Blades of grass are tiny tinder that explode into flames. There are dark storm clouds above but no rain. She watches the grey and orange clouds and smoke and fire from inside her house, which is impermeable to the blaze. She wakes up with a rash on her wrist. Scratches it as she continues her research on her tablet, makes a full list of supplies for the next day.

Her number one live reality show fan, Ron, sits in a new lawn chair with a 7up in one hand and a Molson in the other. He observes her moves, rolling the rototiller down the ramp from the back of the truck to the edge of the yard. It sputters before it starts and at first feels like too much for her to handle. But she steadies her hands, braces her arms, and rolls it across her brown and yellow lawn. The richer earth becomes the top layer. Ron yells things at her as she propels the machine, but she can't hear him, just the roar of domestic destruction. She smiles as she eliminates each crispy blade. It takes all morning just to do one corner. But time doesn't matter. She's satisfied.

Once the grass is gone, and it's just soil, there'll be one more raking session. Val is sure Ron will watch that too. Tear up the grass, smooth the soil, move grass and excess soil with a wheelbarrow to the garbage bin. A little bit each day, she chips away.

In the evenings, she comes inside through the basement door after working and makes sure the curtains are shut. She takes off her striped work gloves, her heavy socks and boots, too hot for this weather, her souvenir Mexico T-shirt, stained with rust, the shorts her husband left behind, too big for her but full of pockets. Her wilted bra, her underwear from a drawer of identical underwear, everything striped. Naked, she gathers the mess and puts it in the washing machine, doesn't turn it on. In the windowless basement bathroom, she stands in the shower stall for too long, just cold water washing over her. She forces herself to scrub head and body with a bar of soap. Head wrapped in a towel, she puts on her robe, starts the wash cycle, eats dinner, watches television, and sleeps on the couch.

Preparing the subbase was no big deal, laying the fine grade stone and compacting it. Even building the form and mesh didn't trouble her. Throughout the early stages, it was work, but she didn't notice. Ron was the only nuisance. Getting her yard torn up wasn't easy, but making the cement is hard. She struggles with the bags of cement, with the old mixer. Her arms feel like saggy grocery bags. It takes three days for her to figure out how to angle the mixer. The consistency wasn't right at all, and that took her longer than she wanted it to.

When she finally pours, she wants to make sure she gets it right. Wants it to look as nice as can be. She smooths it out until it's even. That first section is small but exactly as she pictured it. A test patch.

At night, she celebrates with a couple of beers in the quiet of her living room, television on, muted. The sun goes down, and in the slightly cooler air, she sits in her favourite chair until she's sucked back half a six-pack. She cracks a fourth, one more to help her get some rest. She hears kids running through the alley, the clang of her back gate opening and slapping shut.

In the morning she sees the damage done. Names, initials, hearts, and profanity scrawled. They even left their sticks sitting in the now dry cement. She cracks one off, the nub sticking out, and throws the rest into the alley.

She stretches, puts on her gloves, and fires up the mixer. Ron shouts over the din of the cement mixer, "Can't trust anyone's off-spring these days." She can barely hear him. He's a low buzz. She stares at bags of concrete piled near the shed, checks her watch. The hardware store won't be open for two more hours. Time to whip up another batch before that. She'll call Ben to bring the truck and the alarm company to come on Monday morning.

Usually she hits up the smaller hardware store closest to her. They know her and give her what she's looking for, and they don't ask questions and don't play any music. But they didn't carry anything to break up a solid square of concrete.

In this big chain they have everything, including some terrible radio station. She stalks the aisles trying to find the rental desk.

"Do you need help, ma'am?" A young man with a ponytail asks.

"Rentals."

"Come with me."

Val huffs and follows him. He points to a desk at the far end of the construction section but continues to walk with her until the two of them get there, like she needs a police escort.

"This lady is looking to rent something, Jim."

"Thanks, Cary."

"Glad you two explained everything to each other."

She drops her elbows onto the desk, and Cary and his ponytail leave to escort other customers around the store, like a misguided gentleman.

"I need a saw or something to help me break up a slab of concrete in my lawn."

He stares at Val.

"I'd like it today."

"Okay. So, is this from a patio or some other permanent structure that you're getting rid of?"

"No. It's a piece of my lawn. But some kids vandalized it, and now I need to take out this whole piece and do it again."

He stares at Val.

"I'd like to get back to work as soon as possible, so something like a chainsaw."

"Okay. Do you know how to use this equipment?"

"I don't know what equipment I'll be renting yet, so I don't know if I know."

"Well, some of these tools are more heavy duty than others."

"That's what I want. Something that'll get the job done."

"Will you be using the tools yourself?"

Val raises an arm. He doesn't move. She grabs for a catalogue of items that's attached to the desk and starts flipping through it. She should have just ordered it up on her tablet if she knew she was coming to this place. Then she wouldn't have to talk to any people. Or stare into this man's face while he decides whether or not he's got more useless questions for her.

"Show me something I can use!" Val shouts.

"Mom? Mom?"

She hears Ben's voice. He rounds the corner with Cary and his trusty ponytail.

"Ben, did you bring the truck?"

"Sorry. Yes. Sorry."

"Your mother is looking for something to break up concrete."

"Yes. She needs to undo some damage done. What do you recommend?"

Useless Jim goes back into a storage area and returns with two saws.

"One of these two will do the job well and are a snap to use. It's like slicing off icing on a cake. Sometimes a sledgehammer is good to break up the bigger pieces. And, of course, we also have safety gear too."

"I have—" Val starts to say.

"She has all the safety equipment. I've made sure of it," Ben interrupts.

Val slams shut the open catalogue and stomps up the aisle.

"And a sledgehammer."

"Mom, where are you going?"

"Need more cement. Always need more cement."

Val hauls as many bags as will fit into her trunk to the till. As she loads them in, Ben wheels up a dolly with the saw.

"Thought it would all be a lot more. Bigger. Don't need the truck," she says.

"I can take all of this for you, Mom."

She takes the saw from his hands and straps it into the back seat, clicks the seatbelt to keep it in place.

"Thanks for carrying it out to the car."

Val takes the rest of the day off. Drives her rented saw around town. They pass Ben's elementary school, the playground there already half concrete, for tetherball and square ball next to the basketball court. Up the hill, they cruise by the church where she was married, small and in the middle of a large parking lot. The rink nestled between the river and a parking lot. She drives through neighbourhoods just to feel the pavement under the tires, to watch the shades of grey stretch out in front of her at every turn.

"Excuse me. Is this your house?"

A woman in perfectly creased capri pants mimes knocking on an invisible door next to Val's shrubs.

"Do I look like I live here?"

"Sorry. You can never be sure who's a worker bee and who's not now, can you?"

Val stabs her shovel into the bag of cement. Uses a stick to check the consistency of what's in the mixer. The woman steps to the edge of the area where Val has freshly poured, looks down into the grey wetness.

"Well, I am a representative of the Neighbourhood Enhancement Committee. And we have had a lot of talk about what you're doing here. And we discovered that though it doesn't violate any bylaws, we would like to know, first, what you're doing, and secondly, if you will stop doing whatever it is you're doing."

Val shovels a mound of concrete in a pile in front of the woman. A dollop jumps onto the cuff of her capris. Val shovels another dollop. Ruining the smooth finish of her day's work.

"We would really appreciate if you could come to our next meeting and talk to us about what this is." The woman clutches her purse to her chest, leans back on one leg, and points a circle around all Val's hard work. After her finger travels all the way around, she places her hand on her hip and giggles.

"No."

"Well, if you decline our offer, again, though it's not illegal, we can petition you to restore your lawn to grass, like all of the others in the neighbourhood."

"What's that crazy bitch doing over there, Val?" Ron shouts over from his yard, holds up a Smirnoff Ice, and points with his ice cream sandwich at the woman in the capris.

Val slops more concrete near the woman's sandaled feet. Then she fires up the mixer before telling her, "Get the fuck off of my property."

Once the woman's scoffed and skedaddled, Val arms herself with her steel trowel, fixing her angry mess. Her arms are defined now, and she catches herself watching her arm, marvels at the bulge of her now very visible biceps almost as often as she marvels at the way the grainy mixture turns into an even line. Everything around her is finally starting to look the way it should, and no one seems to appreciate it.

She stands in the alley past the gate, surveys the whole lot. Every space now filled, some still slick and wet, some dry. Something looks wrong. The edge of the lawn along the street is too green, too much life. The shrub along the front street looks absurd. Exhausted, Val leans on the robot-like compost bin. It won't be right unless she does it. She puts her gloves back on and yanks out every plant by every root.

"Val, you're like a machine," Ron shouts, this time an empty bottle his only prop.

Val waves at him. Almost a thank you.

The skies are getting dark, and the man on the weather channel said a forty percent chance of showers. Val drags out thick sheets of plastic, bought just in case of this emergency, and drapes them over the yard. It looks like she's growing something underneath, after all.

She sleeps well. Dreams of clear skies. When she wakes up in the middle of the night, she hears soft rain. The weatherman was right.

It's like Christmas morning. She gets up early, forces herself to stay in bed just a little longer. To hold out. The rain has stopped. The air smells fresh.

Every inch of former grass an unmoving slab. The wall's not quite tall enough but it'll do. Ron won't be blocked out entirely. But something about that feels okay. Ron's a fixture too. Steady and solid, even though he's not doing anything special, only being annoying. But his voice has been her perpetual companion. Even when she's not looking at him, she knows he's there.

She removes the plastic sheeting like she's unwrapping a gift. Underneath beautiful greys, hard and clean. Let them bring their petitions. Let her son come over any time with his kids, and they can have a picnic here. Let him walk up right now and see her in her cement glory and judge her after it's all done. No one can jackhammer a fulfilled dream.

The August sun beats down. She presses her cheek to the wall. So cool. Rolls her body on the concrete lawn. She lifts up her shirt, the front of her pressed to smooth cement. Skin and mortar, clay. Her heartbeat slows for the first time in years. Beats in a slow rhythm. She hears the rush of water as it cascades down a flume, breathes her to life.

Don't Tell Me What to Do

I probably can't drink another shot. But I do. I drink two more. I put my leg up on the side of the pool table and stretch it, even though there's a sign screwed into the side that says "do not sit on pool table!" with a little clip art old man wagging his cane at me. If Gus comes out from behind that bar, I'll just say that I'm not *sitting*; this is stretching, and it's for my better health. Break the rules just enough to annoy.

Gus looks over and makes an angry face. He's old enough to be my dad, but he acts like we were at prom together, close forever. Just because I like music from the eighties doesn't mean we're buddies. I like him, though. He's always making sure the women's washroom is kept clean, and he throws guys out the back door if they're being assholes to me or the other girls who hang out here.

"Alex. We should go home." Robert grabs my hand, but I pull it away.

"Don't tell me what to do."

He knows I hate that more than anything. Being treated like a child, being told what I should do. Like the time he tried to convince me not to bring my half-coffee–half-Bailey's into the movie theatre. No one in this town gives a shit if I want to get a little tipsy while I watch *Spider-Man*.

Robert is old, too. Like, he actually did hang out with Gus at prom. They've been friends for thirty years. They used to live in a basement together before they each got married, then divorced. Robert's been divorced twice. Three times if you count common-law.

I don't care that Robert and Gus both look like they're going to ground me. I run up on stage and grab the mic from the Rocktown Hillbillies frontman. He just laughs, keeps playing "Back in Black." I belt out the lyrics. A group of girls in the back cheer, and I can see them clink their bottles of Canadian together, beer bobbling out the tops. They come up to the front and start singing along, dancing in their short denim skirts and V-neck T-shirts. They're shouting wildly, blocking the small dance floor. Robert is trapped in the corner by the dartboard. I'll come down when I'm ready to drink with these girls, escape into the bathroom to see if anyone has any drugs, any stories, anything fun at all.

"Why did you have to do that?" Gus says. I come out of the bathroom, and he's standing there with a dolly and a keg.

"Why did I have to have a fun time? I don't know. This is a bar." I point to the required poster on the wall telling us to drink responsibly and get a safe ride home. "Where's Robert?"

"He's not a safe ride home." Gus points at Robert, slumped over in a booster seat in the hallway.

I bite at my nails, an old habit I wish I could kick. "I'll have a quiet drink, and we can wait for you to drive us home."

"Can you do anything quietly?"

"Oh yeah." I lean in and whisper in his ear, lips close enough to brush the skin.

Gus drops us off at three a.m. Even though I kept drinking until Gus told me he had to clean the glass I was drinking from, I feel fine. The two of us carry sleepy, boozy Robert from the car, up the steep wooden stairs that connect the alley parking to our back door. I can't get my key to work while trying to keep Robert upright, so we prop him up against the door until I finally get the old lock to click. Robert tumbles to the floor, half inside the kitchen, half outside on the back deck. A rough snort out of one nostril, but he doesn't wake up. Gus gets down and picks him up over his shoulder, walks him into the living room, and sets him on the old sectional. He's stronger than he looks.

Gus eyes up the plywood in place of a countertop. Our kitchen isn't finished. Robert can never pull his shit together, and everything in there is torn apart. We've been cooking with a microwave, a toaster oven, and a barbecue. It's not bad, but the weather is starting to get cold, and Robert hates standing outside in the breeze with his BBQ tongs, and I am constantly charring meat to a blackened crisp when I attempt to grill. I'm not exactly a gourmet cook, but I could put things in the oven if we had an oven. I could make a good tomato sauce if there was somewhere to put a decent-sized pot.

"Do you like what I've done with the place?" I ask Gus.

"Oh, sure. You didn't do this."

"Well, I did put that kettle over there on the floor next to the outlet. How else would I get instant coffee in the morning?"

"I could help Bob with this place. I've told him he can check out my carpentry shed."

I offer him another beer. We might not have much food around, but our fridge is full of beverages. He declines, moves toward the still open door. The fall chill bristles the hairs on my arms.

"Thanks, though," he says.

"Okay then," I say.

Maybe I should have offered him chips and pretzels, my snack-meal staples stashed away at the back of the Lazy Susan.

He's just standing on the deck, staring out at the blue-black night. There are so few lights on, other houses all asleep at this hour. The littlest birds won't be up for another hour or so. No twittering. The crickets aren't even making their quiet racket.

"I don't know what you eat around here," Gus says, "but tomorrow you should come eat at mine. You and Robert. I'll cook. I've got some tricks up my sleeve."

It's gonna rain, and I know he won't want to barbecue in a soaking-wet sweatshirt. "All right, we will. I'll get Robert to pick up some beers."

"No need, Al."

He's the only one who calls me Al. His acting like we're buddies from the glory days, reminiscing about girls we used to pretend to fool around with.

"Okay then. Good night, Gus. See you tomorrow." I'll still force Robert to hit up the liquor store. No sense in being rude.

I reach out for his hand, just want to touch it for a moment. He grips it and gives me a firm handshake. Cups his other hand around too, like this is a serious agreement we've got, an important dinner, where maybe there will be too much beer.

After Gus lets go of my hand, leaves to go across the yard to his own house, I head inside. Robert's yelling for more pillows. I grab two from the spare bedroom and toss them on top of him, place a bucket beside the couch in case he's too lazy to barf somewhere appropriate. He'll pass out again in a minute. I grab the chips, the pretzels, two bottles of beer, and a roll of paper towel. Upstairs in the bedroom, with the curtains open wide, I spread it all out on the bed and eat and drink and stare at the night sky. I wait until the sun crests the mountains, tints the room in orange light, and I can see into the distance.

"Why did you have to make plans without asking me?"

"Gus is your best friend. Fuck."

Robert's been grumpy and on my case since he woke up this afternoon with a hangover, and I told him we needed to get beer for dinner at Gus's tonight. I went on a long walk up and down the streets until I figured he'd be awake and I could use the vacuum. I cleaned the whole place and swept up the sawdust from today's attempt to finish part of the kitchen counter. Even tended to a bloody fingernail he broke while getting angry at a saw. At this rate we'll have a dismantled kitchen until I'm his age.

"Why can't you ever just listen to me?" he says.

"All I do is listen to your mouth sounds all day and night," I say. "You couldn't even carry this beer, because carrying stuff and whining at the same time is too much multitasking."

I knock on Gus's door with a flat palm. He doesn't answer quickly enough, so I burst in, shout his name, "*Gus!*" and run upstairs, yelling his name. I find the kitchen and put the beer into the fridge. Robert slowly clomps up the stairs far behind me. I've never been in Gus's place. For a single guy, it's nice. New fridge, nice dining room table, antique china stacked in a glass cabinet. He's even got photographs on the walls. Never had kids, but his old dog is framed in the living room, along with beautiful bucks, wolves in the meadow, and a large print of the waterfall on the other side of the mountain.

Robert's kids don't talk to him much. I've never even seen them, except once, accidentally. I was driving by the mall along the highway, and Robert was there waving his hands around, trying to wrangle blurry shapes into a car.

Gus comes upstairs with a bottle of wine and pie in a box. He's wearing a button-up shirt that looks ironed, not one of the free T-shirts that comes in a beer box that he usually wears to work.

"Hi, Bob, Alex. Sorry, had to grab a few supplies."

Robert ignores us both and heads to the fridge for beer, grunts something to himself, and gets comfortable on the couch. He probably wants to sit in front of the TV, watch that reality show about hand-fishing and not say another word for the rest of the night.

I turn away from Robert, and Gus motions for us to walk out the sliding glass door. The table is set on the back patio, blue plates, cutlery, wineglasses. Gus has made himself a gorgeous patio set, an umbrella rests in a stand, a firepit of cinder blocks in the shape of a perfect circle. I take the wine from Gus and screw off the top, pour each of us a glass.

"Don't you want a beer?" Gus asks. "I just decided to try this out. Since we're eating deer steaks for supper."

"No, I'll drink this. Save the beer for Robert."

Gus must think I'm like Robert, drinking the same old thing day after day, year after year. Never getting bored of anything when, really, I'm bored half the time I'm not at the bar or working at the Esso. Even at the Esso, I'm bored half that time too. Little halves of my life spent staring into space, trying to figure out how not to be bored.

I sniff the wine like people do to get a sense of it. It smells like the wooden boxes of berries we used to get from our neighbour every summer. I pull the sleeves of my hoodie up around my fingers, grip the wine glass with a cotton-bundled fist. I sip it. Try to take it slow.

"I know it's a bit cold, but I can put on a fire." Gus steps to the firepit, arranges kindling.

I set the glass on the table. Shake it to test how sturdy it is. Solid. I think about what it's like to do things for yourself like that. To know how to make things happen, how to hammer and nail, make something out of little parts, scraps, and pieces. I gulp my wine. The flavours are sweet and tart, and I'm liking it. Maybe I should start making my own wine. I'd be good at selling alcohol.

"I'm starving!" Robert shouts from the living room. He never did manage to put the TV on, just sitting alone with his can of Blue like it's his best friend.

Gus heads inside and by some miracle comes back out ten minutes later with Robert holding a fresh salad. Gus has a bowl of peas and rice and a platter of something juicy and delicious. Robert sits, and Gus takes each of our plates and sets the steak and rice in pretty portions. The food looks even more tempting on the blue plates. I wonder if he thought of that when he was cooking. How to make food pretty.

"Tasty," I say, forkful of rice in my mouth.

"Yeah. Gus, you can cook. No shitting you. Like good." Robert ignores his vegetables like a child, swipes bread into the juice.

We eat quietly. Because it's good food, and because sometimes the three of us together don't have that much to say. Behind Gus's house there are other small houses and their yards. Kids throw a basketball against a garage door. A man collects his children's mess of toys. An old woman snips at her vegetable garden with nail scissors. Some yards empty, just tools and chairs.

"Any excitement with you guys?" Gus asks.

"Besides the renovation, not much. Though that's keeping me pretty busy." Robert says as he fingers the meat, then drops a slice back on his plate.

"It's so boring around here lately," I say, staring at the woman clipping leaves and weeds.

"It's a slow town." Gus fills my glass from the rapidly dwindling bottle of wine.

"There's plenty to do," Robert says, opening another beer.

"Oh yeah?" I say. "There's nowhere fun to go. It would be nice if there was something big around here."

"You gonna talk about that mall again? How can a mall be interesting?" Robert says.

When I was a kid, my mom took us to West Edmonton Mall while we waited for my dad to come back from working up north. This was before he got his job at the pulp mill and lived with us full-time for two years, before he moved one town over and started another family, before my mom gave up on trying to enjoy her life. Before she stopped caring about living.

For three days, my sister and I ate fried foods in the food court and went on waterslides and rides. And, of course, we got cute new things. Discmans, CDs, cool outfits. My mom let us do whatever we wanted, because my dad was coming home with money and we didn't have to worry. We stayed in the Fantasyland Hotel. The room looked and smelled like a tropical island, like a far-away vacation, like someplace beautiful people go to feel even more free.

"That's a nice memory," Gus says.

"It's a stupid mall. Girl dreaming of a mall trip," Robert says, sloshing beer onto his jeans.

"Yeah, that's me. I'm a stupid girl."

"I used to love taking road trips as a kid," Gus says. "The only time we ever got to go anywhere or do anything." He smiles and hands me a slice of bread.

After dinner Robert demands we leave before we even get to the pie, and when I refuse he takes off into the bathroom with a woodworking magazine. Hopefully he'll learn something useful while taking a shit.

"Does wine go with pie?" Gus asks.

I'm a bit tipsy and say, "Wine can go with anything."

"I have one more bottle downstairs in the laundry room."

"I'll go get it," I say.

Downstairs is even cleaner than upstairs. The laundry room doesn't have a thing out of place except for the wine bottle sitting on a box of Tide. Before I head upstairs I snoop in the bathroom, nothing interesting. The main room in the basement is nearly empty. An old stereo on the far wall, speakers in each corner. I walk into the room on what has to be shiny, new wood floors. I slip around on the wood in my socks. Do a skating spin I learned in that one year of lessons. I check to see if things are plugged in, what kind of music Gus puts on in his private den. I drop the bottle of wine, and thankfully it doesn't break. I bend down to pick it up. Kneel a moment, a little light-headed. Perfectly embedded in the floor are circular pieces of metal. I trace my finger around one of the metal circles.

"Are you okay?" Gus is standing in the doorway.

"Yeah. Fine. I dropped the wine." I hold up the still intact red. "It's so neat and clean down here."

He comes over and tries to help me up, but I just stay sitting on the floor, touching the metal, fascinated by the design.

"Come on. Let's go upstairs." Gus seems anxious.

"You don't want me in your precious room? What are these?" I sprawl my body on the floor and reach around me, grab at all the metal rings.

Gus inhales deeply and stands over me. For the first time since I've known him he seems sort of powerful, like I should listen to him.

"They're handles."

"For what? Are these trapdoors?"

I scramble to a sitting position and try to pry one of them open. My long nails make it hard for me to get a decent grip. Gus sits down beside me and pulls on one of the rings. A piece of the floor the size of a cupboard door swings up on an invisible hinge. The wooden floor-doors are so perfectly lined up they look decorative and not functional. Under each is a perfect square hole, also made of wood. Each one houses treasures. We go through every organized section. Neatly organized boxes of photographs. Hockey cards. School medals. Letters from his ex-wife. Metal cash boxes.

"This is incredible. Like, I can't believe this," I say to Gus. He's behind one of the open doors, and I can only see his eyes over the top of the shiny wood. We probably need a third bottle of wine.

"The house is small and I hate clutter. Just wanted somewhere to keep all my things. I got new furniture for down here that'll be delivered in a few weeks. Then this will just look like any other den."

I peek around the side of the door. "What's in those cash boxes?"

He doesn't answer me, examines his impeccable craftsmanship. I crack open the bottle of wine and take a long drink, offer it to Gus. He takes the bottle but doesn't drink. We're sitting on the floor like it's kindergarten show and tell, passing around an adult juice box.

He starts to close the doors one by one. When he gets to the cash boxes I hold it open with all my strength. He tries to move my hand, but I won't budge. I squirm over as close as I can to him without losing my grip. Our bodies are close, and I lean in and bite his ear. He lets go. We kiss, my hands still holding the door open, his hands on either side of him, no other part of us touching. He pulls back and one by one opens the metal boxes. Inside are rolls and rolls of toonies. Hundreds of tight little paper coin rolls bundled together like shiny silver in sleeping bags having the biggest sleepover.

"Holy shit," I say.

I take another swig of wine. Gus does the same.

"Okay. But why so many toonies? A bank doesn't even have so many toonies."

From upstairs, Robert is yelling. I drink as much wine as I can in one gulp.

Gus carefully closes every door and walks over the smooth finish.

"Let's go up, Alex." Gus grabs my hand and doesn't let go until the last possible second before Robert will see our fingers entwined.

At home Robert's on the floor this time. He stumbled in the door before me, and I'm full of wine. Without someone to help me move him I just fold a blanket over him, prop his head up on a stack of magazines, and then get my chips and pretzels, two bottles of beer. It's started to rain. The sunrise won't be visible, but the beats of the rain will hopefully lull me to sleep before then.

I lie. All week. As often as I can, I lie to Robert and go to Gus's on my lunch break, or on my days off. Robert's on shiftwork, and he doesn't pay that much attention to me anyway.

Starting on Monday, I just pop over and he's not even there. I walk into his backyard and sit by the firepit. Stare at the even blocks, the black ash from the fire a few nights ago. I check the basement door. Locked. He must be the only person in town who locks their door. I walk up and down the streets until I get to the bar, join the girls drinking beer late on a work night. We clink our bottles in cheers. Gus isn't behind the bar.

The next day he's home, and I invite myself in. He makes us coffee, and we lay on the living room floor together mostly not talking, barely touching the outside of our hands. His are the slightest bit clammy.

The next day, I walk over at eleven in the evening. Gus is sleeping, but he lets me in and we watch a talk show, and I slink into his lap. After he falls asleep I grab his phone and take a few selfies, only two with my shirt pulled up, my lips puckered in perfect duck face.

Then on Thursday I bring over a bottle of wine, and as soon as I get in the door I take off my shoes and my shirt and walk him straight to the bedroom.

Gus holds me around the waist. It almost seems like he's going to cry, that feeling of his chest quivering a little against mine.

"Bob treats you like—"

"You don't have to say things."

I take his rough hands and put them on my cotton bra cups. He doesn't curl his fingers around them, palms flat, fingers stiff and straight. He looks up into the old ladyish light fixture, a dim bulb.

"He's been my best friend since grade three, and he biked home to get my dad when I fell thirty feet out of our tree fort. I was best man at both of his weddings. And I know he's trying. That last divorce, last set of kids, it wore him out. You must wear him out."

He finally stops talking. I grab the back of his shirt and yank it off. As I fling the T-shirt off, his hands come apart from my boobs for a second, but he places them back right away, like he doesn't want to offend me.

"Move in with me. You can take the spare room even. He's my friend, but I don't want to see you in that house with him. He's confused and just can't be responsible for another woman right now. Do it. Listen to me."

We make out with no tops on, like two teenagers scared to take off any more clothes because someone's parents should be getting home any minute. He's the one who stops, tells me not to take my jeans off. He takes one hand and reaches into his jeans pocket and folds two newly cut keys into my palm.

Things move fast with these middle-aged guys. They're used to being married, even if they've been divorced for ten years, like Gus. I fell asleep in my bra and jeans, and now it's well beyond sunrise and I've been out all night. The keys to Gus's place rattle around in my almost empty purse. It's my day off, so I head home to sleep all day. Robert's already at work when I get in. There's a full pack of empties on the deck.

I wake up at three in the afternoon and look into my open closet. The rolling suitcase I moved in with is still sitting there, underneath a pile of T-shirts and shorts from when it was warm enough to let my legs breathe. Four months ago, I'd thought this wouldn't be the great romance of my life and that it wouldn't last. And I was right about both of those things, but I had my own bed to crawl into, and the house wasn't far from work. When I moved in there was a kitchen countertop, and Robert smelled of the fruity woman's body wash his wife had left behind six months earlier. He was raw but sweet. That must have been what both of his wives fell in love with. I didn't fall in love with anything. I liked that he was always up to meet me for a drink, didn't question why I never went back to the house with my bitchy roommates, didn't say a word when I rolled my shit into the bedroom upstairs and didn't leave.

When Robert storms into Gus's wood shop that evening and finds his arms around my waist, his hands on my hands pushing a slab through the planer, I almost let my hand go through too. Gus steps back, and I pick up another piece of wood, tap it against a pile of sawdust, send a little cloud into the air. I know just what to say.

"I thought Gus could teach me a thing or two, so I could help you with the renovation."

The buzz of the wood getting smaller is probably what my voice sounds like to Robert's ear right now. His face tenses, one eye shrinks to the size of a dime. That's how angry he is. He's going to lose an eye to rage.

"I don't need help. You insulting me?"

Gus jumps in. "I'm not insulting anything, Bob. Alex just wants to learn."

"I'm not blaming you, Gus. This one, she is always trying to make me look stupid."

"The kitchen has been in ruins for three months," I say. "Maybe you need an expert. Like Gus."

Robert kicks the sawdust pile. Gus turns off the machine.

The only sound is everyone breathing heavy.

"Maybe I could help you," I say again. "You don't let me do anything."

Robert moves to grab my arm, but I slam the two-by-four against the floor. I slam it again, and again, then drop it. I look at Gus first. He's staring at me, looks tense, but he doesn't move. Robert stares at the unmoving band saw in the corner. I walk over to Robert and grab his arm, lead him out into the backyard. I look behind me, mouth "one hour."

I convince Robert I'll meet him at the bar. That I need to shower all the dust and wood and sweat off my body. I strip in the hallway and promise I won't go behind his back again, that I won't get in his way with construction. That he's got this. I turn on the shower and wait for the clunk of the door shutting. I turn off the water and run upstairs, put on my favourite jeans, T-shirt, and hoodie, and grab my suitcase waiting in the closet.

Robert's car is parked up the street because his construction supplies take up all of the carport and part of the alley. He doesn't lock the doors. The spare car keys were still in the fishbowl in the unfinished basement bathroom.

I park a street up from Gus. He's on a steep hill. When I get inside he looks relieved, like maybe I wasn't going to show up. His arms wrap around me, like he's trying to protect me from something. He just holds me there for a long time. I push my open eyes into his chest, look at the plaid fabric of his shirt up real close. Then he's grappling with my belt, and I guess he was protecting me from his raging boner, which I feel through his jeans and which probably got harder because he was holding me so close. He was too awkward in the bedroom, so I wrestle him to the floor of the living room. Our naked bodies bristle on the carpet. Gus is so gentle. His hands roll over my skin so lightly that he might as well be across the room. He moves like I'm made of glass. I imagine Robert judging us both for being total sex wusses, for not rattling the house until it falls down. His delicate thrusts are too respectful.

"Tell me about the toonies," I say, biting his ear.

"What?"

"Tell me all about your fat rolls of toonies," I whisper. Grind against him.

"I have so many toonies," he says. Flips me over onto my back and takes control.

"So hot," I say.

"How much money? Tell me about the money." I roll him back over so I'm on top.

He just groans, and I pull back, slow down. "Don't make me stop. How much, Gus?"

"Over thirty-five grand." He groans again, and I speed up.

"Holy fucking shit." I rock him to completion and collapse.

"We're like two loonies that make a toonie," he mumbles.

"Thanks, Gus. That means a lot coming from you."

I go to bed before the sunrise for once, Gus's arm draped over me and his clean striped quilt. I try to wait to see slivers of light from behind the curtains, but my eyelids dip and I sink into sleep. His bedroom window faces north anyway.

In the morning, Gus has to go in to wait for deliveries. I'm pretending to be asleep. Before he gets out of bed he strokes my cheek, rubs each finger over the apples, and doesn't say anything. It's nice, and I keep my eyes closed, stay so still. He kisses my fingers and quietly puts on his Labatt's T-shirt and jeans and slips out the front door.

The second he's out the door I toss the covers off myself, dress, and head downstairs with my suitcase. The main room in the basement looks even prettier in the morning light, the wood grain shining. Gus must have just polished the floor. In the front pocket of the suitcase, I've stashed Robert's screwdriver. The one he threw into the yard when he couldn't quite get a light switch cover to cooperate. I thought I'd remember exactly which hidey-hole had the toonies, but I pop open two with the screwdriver before I see the matte grey cash boxes.

Each roll feels heavier than a can of beer. I reach into the first case and fill each hand, let the money sit there, perfectly neat and packaged. They look like cute little gifts. I can't take them all, but I fill the case so I can still actually carry it without putting my back out. No time to count, but I probably have eight grand. I close every cash box, stack them back in order, close the wooden lid, and rub clean every surface I've touched with the sleeve of my hoodie.

I totter up the hill with the heavy case dragging behind me. It feels like it barely has wheels at all as I scrape the bottom along the dusty concrete, keep having to set it upright as I struggle to get it to the car. I grab seven rolls and drop them in my purse. Knees bent, I inhale deeply into my lungs, shove my arms underneath the bottom of the case and get it halfway into the open trunk. Sweat drips into my eyes. I put all my weight on the case to keep it from falling. A nice man walking his dog offers to help me as I heave the case into the trunk. I decline, say fuck a few times, and topple my whole body onto the suitcase, which thankfully ends up thudding into the trunk. Then I pat his pit bull and climb into the driver's seat.

I try not to speed, even though all I want is to get somewhere fast. If Robert reported his car stolen, then I'm in big trouble sooner. But he hasn't been driving lately, since he's been drinking so much, and he walks up the hill to work. He's supposed to pick up his kids on the weekend, so hopefully I can get three days of driving in before he gets super suspicious. He might bail on those kids anyway. He's reliable that way.

First stop is the mall in Cranbrook. New outfits. I need some. Why bring clothes when your goal is to steal a shit ton of toonies that you can spend, spend, spend. New jeans, not on sale, that cost over a hundred dollars. Slim T-shirts that fit perfectly. A black leather jacket and a wool jacket the colour of fresh blood. I get two dresses, decide I will treat myself to a sit-down dinner as soon as I get to West Edmonton Mall. One pair of heels, one pair of sneakers, and a bigger black purse made of real leather are the last things I buy before taking a quiet minute in the women's washroom. I come out wearing my new black jeans, grey T-shirt, and leather jacket. It looks like a sexy criminal's uniform from a movie. Underneath I'm wearing new underwear, black lace everything.

I buy myself an iPhone, fling my shattered android into the trash can along with my old clothes, before I head to the food court. I toss two coins to the kid at Taco Time for toonie Tuesday and spend another at Dairy Queen for an Oreo Blizzard. I stop by the liquor store on my way out and buy a 26 of rye. I keep my favourite hoodie, put it on the seat next to me as I drive, an old friend. We're on the lam together.

At the motel, I turn on the television. I didn't want to start getting too fancy until I got to the real destination, but the place had a big sign flashing free cable, and I'd almost driven the car into a semi two hours ago. I want to be fresh when I get to the mall, and a few hours of sleep would help. But when I crawl into my glamorous Roman-themed bed, I won't want to get out for days.

The pop machine outside the lobby is too old to take toonies, but luckily I've got other change from my purchases. I load up on ginger ale and ice. Drop another buck for Hawkins Cheezies. I fill the sink with ice, unwrap a plastic cup, and fill it with rye, spritz the top with ginger ale. Then I put on *So You Think You Can Dance* and strip my new clothes off to the theme music. On the edge of the nightstand, I crack open two paper rolls like eggs and spray the silver and gold coins onto the bed. In my new La Senza underwear I jump on the bed, let them ting and clink around me. I roll around, let the coins stick to my skin, hold up handfuls and let them slap down on my body. A muscular, young black guy and a tiny white girl dance to Drake. "Started from the Bottom (Now We're Here)." I laugh and crack open another roll, let the coins cascade onto my naked belly.

I know I should get to a bank, change this money into paper. I wonder if Gus has these rolls marked somehow. Even though he's as organized as hell, I don't think he ever imagined anyone would steal his toonies. All night, the TV flickers without sound. I dream of a bright, open sky, purple- and pink-like flowers suspended in air.

The Fantasyland Hotel won't take cash. I need a credit card. A woman with makeup that looks like a sprayed beauty queen mask tells me this, and I try not to punch her fake eyelashes off her face. My new purchases and the money roll behind me in my old suitcase. Now that I've been denied Fantasyland, the little plastic tires feel like they're leaving a trail of black tar behind me. I won't be going upstairs into a Roman bath, with a glass of booze and a fluffy robe waiting on the arm of a marble statue.

I walk by the huge replica of Columbus's *Santa Maria*. Nearby there are submarines indoors, and that makes me still think that anything is possible. I sit in the food court to think. I order a Coke and a giant tub of fries smothered in everything, and I eat it all, even the slimy green onions. It's exactly what I wanted: creamy, salty, spicy, crunchy, gooey. As many flavours and textures that could fit into a paper bowl, be scooped with a plastic fork, washed down with bubbly sugar.

I'd heard stories about people living in the mall, that there's an entire task force of security monitoring and trying to remove people from here. A guy told me that a girl lived for two months in a condemned storage room at the Brick. He also said she ate Cinnabon every day, but that seems unlikely. It's easy to get tired of Cinnabon. That's not what I want to do with myself, but I could see a few days of crashing in here until I get things sorted out.

I find Bourbon Street, with its neon lights and bright colours, and head straight to the Tony Roma's. Rolling up with this suitcase not only looks more ridiculous the longer I do it, but it's also starting to take its toll on my arm. The throb pulses down to the wrist. Every ten minutes I'm switching hands so my biceps won't be uneven. I don't want one bodybuilder's arm. That's how stupid people get caught. And by spending dozens of toonies like it's a normal thing to do.

"Table for one please, ma'am." I smile at the hostess as though I'm selling something.

"Okay, I could do for six p.m. or eight p.m." This girl in her tight black dress isn't smiling, just looking cautiously over the long sheet of names.

"Six. I'm meeting someone later. My husband. That's why I've got this suitcase. I forgot my credit card, so I guess he needs to check us in."

"Mm hm. Okay, six will work great. Now, did you know

that there's a place to check your bag? You could always leave it in one of the storage lockers."

"Oh, it's full of very precious cargo. Personal items that it would be impossible to replace. It'd be a real tragedy." I thrust my huge purse onto the desk, and two rolls of toonies jump out and bang into a stemmed glass of water. The girl grabs the glass and lets the rolls of coins slam to the floor. I bend to pick them up, toss them into my dangling purse.

"Mm hm. Well, that's fine then. We'll see you and that suitcase at six p.m." She smiles and tilts her head like a dog I should give a treat to.

Instead I just smile back like I'm the fanciest fuck in the world and hoist my heavy coin-filled purse onto my shoulder. I have more purchases to make. Accessories, makeup, a box of Band-Aids in case my feet blister in my new shoes. And I have to figure out where I can get a credit card, how I can sort this money into paper and plastic before it gets me in trouble.

I check the screen on my brand new iPhone. Almost four p.m. I need to find a bank. I walk a huge section of the mall, first just trying to find one of those ugly directory maps. I pass the ice rink, keep walking, almost stop in another food court even though I'm holding out for my Tony Roma's ribs. Dolphins, fountains, huge mall sculptures. The amusement park looks too shiny, and if I didn't have to take a suitcase full of toonies on with me I'd ride the Mindbender, shake loose some of this stress. When I do find a directory, I'm overwhelmed with how huge the map is, how far away a bank seems to be from where I am, how the mall seems so much larger than my whole town. How can there not be more banks, when some of the same stores are listed on the map three times?

I root around in my new purse to make sure my wallet is still in there, then race toward the nearest bank. My arms and legs are starting to feel tight and hot. Teen girls in groups block my path, and I slip past them. My story is that I have an eccentric aunt, and she gave me all of these toonies. A family of six with two double strollers takes up all the room between kiosks, but I dodge them. I whip through a group of old people getting their mall walk exercise. My story is that my eccentric aunt died in an eccentric way. All her ceramic figurines crashed on her in her sleep and suffocated her, and I inherited a huge chest from her home, and it was filled with toonies.

I can see the warm green of a bank logo in the distance. There will be people in blouses and button-up shirts in there whose jobs are probably to ask a lot of questions. The only bank account I've ever had was opened for me by my mom at the local credit union when I was fourteen. My story is ridiculous. I *wish* I had a rich, eccentric aunt.

I backtrack to a money exchange I passed earlier and get them to change six rolls into six fifties. An amount that doesn't seem too suspicious. Like, maybe I just emptied a piggy bank I've had all my life. My ankle is blossoming into a blister, so I sit and watch people go up and down escalators. Then I remember I have a phone that works, and I add more apps. By the time I make it back to the bank, people in blouses and dress shirts are pulling closed the metal gate, locking it up for the night.

With an hour until my fancy dinner I shuffle through the mall, buy red lipstick, liquid eyeliner, and a rhinestone necklace that looks like it could choke me. I take everything into the washroom with me, get ready while women have a last-minute piss before they go to their waiting homes or hotel rooms.

I tuck a tissue into my shoe to deal with the pain and, with no real plan, walk to the hotel. Maybe I can leave a cash deposit, pretend my husband is trapped in a tiny airport with no way of getting out for the night. Then I could get everything figured out in the morning.

When I walk into the lobby, there's a new woman at the desk, hair long and shiny. And she's talking to a man who's got the exact same tiny half-moon bald spot as Gus. My face tightens. He could have flown here this morning. Or afternoon. Two flights a day into Edmonton from that shitty airport. I turn and almost take out a toddler with the suitcase as I rush away as fast as I can.

In my new heels and the sexier of my new dresses, black and backless, I sit in the lounge and wait for my table to be ready. My suitcase is stored underneath the bar, my legs clipped underneath, crossed at the ankles, always in contact with the full bag. If Gus is in this mall, he won't know where to find me. The hotel was his only clue.

The guy at the M A C counter had given me a whole new face, and I paid for every tube and tub, brush and bronzer he used. He was so pretty, and he made me look like I oozed glamour. The lipstick was called Pure Fantasy, and the orange hue made my lips like a summer sky. I puckered, took a selfie with my new phone. I wish I could Facebook it, but that would be too obvious. I'm no genius, but I know I can't go doing that.

As I sip my cocktail, the happy hour special with a shot on the side, two mall cops stroll by, their little radios buzzing away with words and codes that don't mean anything to me. I should have spent more time with Robert, listening to the police scanner. They ignore me. I kick the suitcase, but it's already as far in the dark under the bar that it can be.

I hope those two assholes didn't conspire together. If Gus showed up here alone, that's fine. I could take Gus ratting me out. He deserves to. And I bet he'd still forgive me. That loveable bastard. But Robert. He owes me. A car is a small price for that juicy slice of my youth, his bitchery, the sounds of his unskilled carpentry.

The same girl with the black dress and mm hms from earlier comes over and tells me that my table will take a little longer. Asks if I want an appetizer. I do. I dip calamari in creamy sauce. Deep fried seafood is a perfect food group.

Now the mall cops are on the other side of the bar. Everything in here is so visible, so easily identifiable. Even though it's still early, I feel as if I could fall asleep already if someone picked me up and tucked me into bed.

When I was a kid, I remember going into a women's clothing store here. It was the first time I wasn't in a store for kids or a department store. The clothes were so adult. I could picture women's bodies filling them out, their skin peeking from the top and the bottom, hair cascading down backs to meet zippers. This dress I'm wearing, these shiny green shoes, they're what I pictured all women wore. I was allowed to buy one outfit, and it was too big, but that didn't matter. The blouse was cute and professional, the little skirt short and flirty. I wore it to school, even though everyone else was in crewnecks and jeans that fit them properly. I loved how I looked, that I'd picked it out myself. When a girl made fun of me after gym class, called me a lady loser, I punched her in the leg. She screamed that ladies don't punch, and so I punched her other leg to prove that they did.

The mall cops are talking to the Mm Hm Girl at the front; she moves her arm to point. I'm staring straight at her. She motions for them to go behind a partition. I take my shot. I drop calamari down my throat like I need it to live. I order another drink to calm my nerves. The girl goes back to her podium to greet people. I don't see mall security.

Robert's car isn't down in the mall parkade. I was too worried to keep it close to me for another day. Parked it by the side of the road and walked in my leather jacket, even though I was freezing. Looking cool feels good, warms the soul. Good riddance anyway. Don't need anything of Robert's anymore. Sweet Gus's toonies are with me. Shiny starts to a new life. The mall is so anonymous. No one should know me here, but if I don't get these toonies sorted out now my life won't ever change. If I get caught though, this time I won't be able to snake my way out of it.

Mall cops walk out the front door, and I'm glad I got another drink; I take a triumphant sip. The Mm Hm Girl is talking to someone else now and looking down at a phone. Out from behind the partition steps a man and his bald spot. My chest squeezes my heart, my lungs. It might be easier to be alive if you knew you could force your own ribs to puncture your organs at will. Is it Gus? It has to be. Even from a distance I can see he's concerned. I can tell that look in his eyes, his look of wanting to help.

I slink along the short wall separating the booths, ask the bartender where the bathroom is. He points into the main part of the restaurant, near the kitchen. Ignoring the tall wooden door with a sign that says "ladies," I scoot into the kitchen. I run in my heels, pulling the suitcase, don't look or stop as people shout that I'm not supposed to be there. I click through the kitchen until I'm out the back door, in a long hallway that leads to the back rooms of other stores. I wait quietly behind a cart of folded T-shirts until someone comes along and pulls it through a door, then I wedge my toe to keep the door open and slip inside.

I bump into a perfectly put-together woman in chinos, with a walkie-talkie.

"You can't be back here," she snaps. "This is our stockroom."

"I'm so sorry," I say. "I got lost on the way from the bathroom."

"It's strange how often this happens. Come out this way, please."

She leads me through a room of bags and belts and out into the store, and I thank her. The suitcase is wearing me down. If I can get enough money into my purse I can ditch it. Earlier I should have exchanged more rolls for paper cash.

Everything is brightly lit, so clean and fresh. I probably need a new outfit and to get out of these heels and this dress. If I need to run again, I should throw my hair into a ponytail. Grabbing as many slim pants and denim and cotton things as I can, I head into the fitting room and lock the door. I decide I'll spend as long as I can trying everything on, looking at my new appearance. I struggle to get out of the dress because the zipper's stuck.

"Fuck, fuck, fuck, fuck, fuck, fuck."

The fucks don't release the teeth of the zipper from the lining of the dress. These pants would look so chic and slim; in these shirts I could look like anyone else, someone on vacation somewhere hot.

I start to peel off the black dress, pull hard to get it over my head, but it tears as I bring the waist over my shoulders. I hang it on the nice wooden hanger, frayed fabric and loose threads burst from the rip along the middle. I didn't look at myself enough times before I ruined it, and now I'll never get to wear it again. Maybe Gus had seen me from the back as I slipped through the swinging kitchen door. Admired me as I escaped. My ass in a tight black dress, waving goodbye. Maybe it hadn't been him at all.

Except he probably won't just let me leave like that. Came all the way here looking for me. Fuck him for actually listening to my dreams. At least Robert had the common decency to ignore me.

The lightest-coloured khakis are the first thing I grab. I pull them on along with a tight, white V-neck tee. It's so clean and fresh. In the mirror, I see a different girl. Definitely someone who's not me. A person who orders coffee with very specific instructions about temperature and caffeine and foam. Someone who owns a forty-dollar water bottle. Someone who knows how to put on all of this makeup perfectly herself, every single morning.

My eyes feel fuzzy. "Fuuuuuuuck," I intone quietly.

An employee knocks lightly on the door.

"Hi there. Are you doing okay with everything? Do you need any other sizes?"

"No thanks." I try to sound like a chipper shopper.

She shuffles away to help other customers. I push all the clothes I haven't tried on into a pile on the floor. I roll myself into the pile of pale shirts and soft denim. This is a brief rest. I wish I'd taken a few more bites, one more shot at Tony Roma's. I could have savoured the flavours while I waited out that very nice man I robbed. The one I don't want to be with, no matter how kind he is, how much he cares about me. He looked at me like it was hard to look at me, like he felt too much. The fuzziness in my eyes feels like when you're in a dream and you can't cry, but you think if you could then you'd be okay after all.

I stretch out my legs, knock the suitcase over on top of my legs. It hurts. I kick it off and sit up. Blisters on my feet, and now there will be bruises on my legs. In the mess of clothes, I unzip the suitcase, drop rolls of coins into the purse. To make sure I'll still be able to walk without crashing over to one side, I stand up and walk around in the little square of the fitting room, do a jumping jack. I add a sweater and a dark denim jacket to my outfit. Only my scraggly hair still looks like me.

On the walk to the cash register, I push the suitcase behind a rack of men's plaid shirts. It physically hurts to let it go. I buy a V-neck in every colour, a pair of jeans, plain canvas shoes. I explain that my dress ripped and that I'll need to wear these clothes out. I pay for them with toonies, my last big toonie hurrah purchase, and I ask if I can go back into the change room to undress and cut off the tags. She loans me a pair of scissors.

After I've taken off the clothes, cut the price tags, and handed them over the door, I look at myself in the mirror. I whip my hair into a ponytail, gathering it all in one hand, and hack at it with the scissors. I stuff the hair into my purse, heavy with toonies, and zip it up. I layer myself in new clothes, two full bags of things that I would never normally wear sitting on the change room bench beside me. I grab them and my purse and head out the door. My shoulder throbs with the weight of it all, but in the fake light of the mall I feel light, fresh, and ready to run.

Miss Supreme

At the hair salon, Carol Winter looks at Sashay as if she were a dollar store Barbie. She smirks at the little girl and struts out the door, fingers flipping her fresh bob before Linda has a chance to tear out a chunk of Carol's newly tinted hair. Sashay did her own styling today—swiped mascara across her lashes, dabbed sky blue along the lids to spark her grey eyes. A smear of Tulip Bliss lipstick dots one of her teeth, small, crooked nubs with gaps between. The whole look is charming. Carol sucks, judging a child with her eyeballs like that.

"Can't you make her hair any bigger?" Linda asks.

Rhonda, their long-time hairdresser, sighs, brushes an errant tendril behind Sashay's ear. Bulbs of curl sprawl across Sashay's head. Butter blonde strings hold a can of hairspray, but still, her scalp is visible, hair too thin to tease to high heaven. Linda knows this, that Sashay didn't inherit her full locks, got her father's wispy hair. Sashay flicks her tongue at her reflection.

"With extensions. Or a full wig," says Rhonda.

"Sashay do you want a wig or extensions?"

Sashay grabs Linda's hand and pets it, gives it a wet kiss.

"I want big hair like Mama. I want to win. Are we almost

done? This chair is making my butt itch."

Rhonda's committed to Sashay's hair and prepping her for the Miss Supreme Pageant. They've only ever participated in small-time local pageants before. This one has some prestige. It's in a hotel, not the legion hall, in a big city, with 150 girls in mascara and expensive gowns. But Sashay is loveable and spunky. She just has a hair problem.

Rhonda did Linda's hair for a pageant in high school, a French twist, which looked simple and clean but wasn't bold enough. It paled next to the other girls' bouffants, not to mention their rhinestone-encrusted dresses and bleached teeth. Linda placed third runner-up in the Miss Jewel City pageant. No money, a small tiara, the smallest throne at the back of the float. She'd lived in the same town ever since, with the third-best lawn on the block.

The last of Linda's vacation money was sunk into the dental flipper, a set of perfect teeth to fit over Sashay's missing baby and new grown-up ones. It's something they can't do without. Glitz pagaents mean no gaps. Kevin's health benefits are pretty good, but the Chiclet-white fake teeth are considered a nonessential. The insurance provider didn't think her argument that they were for Sashay's career counted as a medical reason. Instead of a trip to their family dentist, she drove Sashay in secret to a specialist while on a dress-shopping trip. Sashay can't be expected to parade around on stage with her real teeth. She might as well get on stage, pee in a sandbox, and smear melted crayons on her clothes.

At the till, Linda hands over a bottle of homemade Chardonnay and some blondies, the only appropriate baked good payment for a hairdresser. Rhonda hugs Linda and the bottle. Linda has time to figure out what barter to bring next week for her own bold highlights and cut. Thin as it is, Sashay's hair is the perfect flaxen shade, and Linda dyes her own to match. Still in the hairdressing gown, Sashay jumps out of the chair and runs into Linda's arms, scattering snips of hair everywhere.

Kevin shakes her in the middle of the night.

"What is this bill?"

The flipper. Linda pretends to sleep. Holds the blankets to her face tight, almost suffocating. She imagines his pride, seeing Sashay hold her bouquet, crown sparkling on her head, the $500 prize money fanned out in front of her perfect little face. A winner.

"I thought you said the dress was $300?"

"Did I?" It's not the flipper bill.

"This says $350. The pageant budget is out of control."

She jumps out of the covers, skitters to the edge of the bed. "I know. I'm sorry. She also needs extensions."

"No. She can use her real hair."

"But—"

"No, Linda. No."

Hands clenched to his boxers, she tugs them down, works her tongue and mouth until he says yes. The next morning she gets up to find a note. *Sorry to be tough on you. No more money on this pageant.* He's left thirty dollars for groceries.

Sashay was an angel at the spray tan salon. The ladies gave her a special rate and a treat. She munches the Snickers Fun Size in the doorway of the post office. Linda pops open the PO box to find a small package. Sashay's eyes get big when she sees the box.

"This is for you, Sassy."

"Is that earrings, Mama?"

Since getting her ears pierced for her fifth birthday, Sashay asks for earrings every time they enter a store. At the supermarket, at the bakery, at the hardware store. Her eyes pop like a lizard when she sees shiny things and tidy boxes. The dresses she wants always have the most sparkle.

Linda opens the box. Nestled in padding and a sealed and sterilized plastic bag is Sashay's flipper.

"It's not jewels. It's your flipper, princess."

"Ooooh! I wanna try it on."

Wide mouthed, Sashay waits, tapping her toes in rhythm with her talent routine dance number. With a steady hand, Linda tries to lock it in place. It fits. Cheeks stretched in a near smile, Sashay grimaces.

"Your face will get used to it. I promise."

"Hi, Mrs. Shue," says Sashay to their mailbox neighbour, slurring, spitting, and practising blowing kisses.

"Hello, there."

The woman looks down at the fake teeth and up to meet

Linda's eyes. "Your daughter does those pageants."

"Yes."

"These are my new teeth!" Sashay hisses.

"I see that, Sashay. Like that reality show. So offensive. No offense. My niece from Fernie drove all the way to Calgary for one a month ago. Cost my sister a fortune, but they have money to waste on dressing like cupcakes and strippers."

Linda plucks the flipper from Sashay's mouth, wipes saliva on her jean shorts, and carefully puts the flipper back in the bag and then into the padded box.

"Sashay is building character. And learning so much."

"Of course. My daughter's going to be in the provincial spelling bee."

"Does she have to be on stage for that? For all eyes to see?"

Linda plunges her fist into her coat pocket, the box in her firm grip. Taking Sashay's hand, she stomps out to their parked car. Sashay wipes her spitty palm on Linda's bare leg.

Linda drops Sashay off at Rhonda's for pageant practice: poise training, finger pointing, pouting and smiling, walking and turning, the subtle art of dancing with your hips without gyrating too much.

She takes side roads nearest the mountains, engulfed in trees. Two towns over is still close enough for people to know who she is, but there will be more strangers, a higher percentage of people who don't know she sells insurance part-time in a strip mall.

Linda ransacks the dollar store, fills her plastic basket with phony ponytails, clip-on strips of plastic hair. The final price is less than twenty dollars. Enough left over to make a payment on the flipper before Kevin sees the bill, hidden in her underwear drawer.

Linda strokes the hairpieces, waxy and obviously fake. This might be the last time Sashay will be like this, Linda's little buddy, Mama's girl. Soon she'll be at school, and they won't be together as much. She'll find new things to love, new friends, new excitement. Her spunk will give her so many ideas. Linda will still be exactly where she is now.

They sit together at the computer. Kevin is mad about the cheap hair too. He doesn't understand that otherwise she won't be competitive.

"You've never spent this much before."

"Those pageants were low stakes."

"Do you even know what you're doing?"

Linda plays montage after montage. Girls in their enormous glowing hair, winning trophies as big as their bodies. The judges, their words cutting, their praise only for participants with the most polished looks. *Frizzy hair, unkempt, raised in a barn, disgraceful, sad.*

Kevin looks like he has the worst case of heartburn on record.

"We've already spent the money. We need her to be her best. We can't humiliate our own daughter. Do you think she's not good enough? Do you think she's not worth it? Don't you want her love?"

He doesn't answer, turns off the computer monitor.

"We've just got to go all in and be there. You have to be there."

He runs a hand through her unwashed hair.

Kevin and Sashay watch cartoons in the living room. It's close to dinnertime, but Linda is on a deadline. In the laundry room, she shoves an embroidery needle through the segments of bleachy hair until the edges form a semi-circle, or something slightly larger than a semi-circle. Then she takes more long curls and adds them to the base, over and over again. She keeps piercing her fingers. Seamstress wasn't on her resumé, but she has to keep going, has to fit in this craft project while making sure they have clean clothes for the day trip.

"Honey, I'm starving over here."

"Me too, Mama."

Knuckles stiff, she takes the last track of hair and threads, makes sure it's as tight as possible. Careful not to smear blood on the light hair, she sets it down on the foam head and washes her hands in the wide laundry tub, wraps her hands in two clean towels, and carries her creation into the living room.

She presents it to Kevin and Sashay. Sashay strokes the curls, pulls them like a pig's tail, and lets them snap back.

"Wow," Kevin says.

"Is that for me?"

"Of course."

"I love you, Mama," Sashay says as she burrows into Linda.

They're running late, and the car seat won't clip, broken clasp. Another thing she forgot to fix, can't replace just yet. Instead of trying to fix it, Linda plunks Sashay down in the back seat, straps the seat belt on. The neighbour's dog shit in their carport, and Linda stepped in it. Rhonda cancelled at the last minute because some kid at the salon gave her strep. The fake hair wig concoction sits on a Styrofoam wig stand in a Styrofoam-filled box in the trunk, and they don't have a hair expert to fix it. Rhonda was against the homemade wig from the start.

The drive is long and hot, and she's paranoid that the costumes will be wrinkled, that there won't be a steamer, that Sashay will vomit at some point in the next eighteen hours. Kevin is driving them so that she can coach Sashay with focus. On the way back they'll nap together in the back seat, after a fast food stop for burgers in crinkly paper, a pee break.

Kevin drops them off to park the car. In the hotel lobby, Sashay runs to a little girl decked out in a purple tracksuit. Large gems spell out "Jewel" on the back. She's wearing sunglasses. Her parents are nowhere in sight.

"Hi, Jewel!"

"Your mom smells like dog farts."

Sashay looks confused, hurt, then softens to Jewel's giggle, relents to the hilarity of dog farts. Linda wants to be angry at Jewel's rudeness but is more annoyed at the accuracy of her nose.

Linda ushers Sashay into the ballroom to register. Politeness and decorum, signing papers, and obtaining nametags. Her daughter eyes the tourists rolling suitcases in and out of the elevators.

"Are we going to sleep in a hotel room?"

She's told Sashay many times they are not going to sleep in the hotel. They'll drive back tonight. They'll survive the day on snacks in her purse.

"We have to hurry. There isn't much time."

Since they don't have a hotel room, they're stuck with the washroom. There's a dressing room for prep, but when they walked by, it was already cluttered with hot rollers, screaming kids, and racks and racks of dresses. She can't focus on perfection when there is so much going on. Linda works fast, and Sashay sits frozen on the toilet seat. Makeup goes on with only a little fuss. The hair stayed perfect, the Styrofoam peanuts a cloud of cushion. As she affixes the pins, a strand of artificial hair breaks off. A minor glitch. She holds the strand, dotted with glue, to Sashay's head until it seems secure.

A girl in frothy buttercup tulle runs through the washroom and into a stall.

"Mom! My butt is so angry!" she shouts to no one visible. Frat-a-tat explosions rumble from her tiny body, a stream of splashes quickly follow. "My butt!" she shouts again.

A moment later, a woman in high heels and yoga pants clicks in on the tile floor and looks around with worry. Linda points to the stall, and the woman slides in with her child. The two of them whisper to each other over the other, more audible, noises.

Linda scoops up Sashay's dress, and instantly her daughter's arms go up over her head. With precision, she shimmies it onto her body, zips up the back, and fastens the hook and eye; then Sashay turns around to face her. Sashay's dress looks beautiful, shimmery sky blue with silver stars and rhinestones on the bodice, the layers of her skirt as bouncy as her hair, finished off with a silver belt of gems. Her fake teeth bright as sunshine. Even in the bathroom lights, Sashay looks lovely and perfect. Linda wants to snap a good photo, but Kevin has the camera bag with the fancy camera with him. It would have been another thing for her to carry. She snaps a quick photo with her phone and stops before uploading it to social media. It feels like bad luck.

"Are you ready?"

Without a word, Sashay struts out to the competitors' entrance, turns at the last moment, and waves proudly. No hug, no need for encouragement. Linda takes the shedded fake hairs and forms a small ball in her hands.

In the audience the mothers whisper, tell jokes. Linda read online that the most famous pageant girl retired at the age of six. On the day she announced her retirement, her Facebook fan page filled with death threats and calls for the girl to commit suicide. Linda admired the girl's mother, the way she went on *Good Morning America* and told people to stop hating on a little girl.

Her daughter will make lots of money and be famous and loved. More people love her than send anonymous hate posts on the internet. Linda knows this must be true. A blonde doll of a girl is born to be admired.

Kevin stands behind their seats in the conference room, proud in his "Sashay Sashays" T-shirt. After just two tries, the iron-on printer paper worked for them, Linda and Kevin together in the basement last night, their daughter asleep upstairs, unaware of this surprise that might not work out.

"I can't get her face to not look like a pug's," Linda said, picking at an image of her child with one eye and a peeling nose stretched across a yellow shirt.

"Give me the iron," he says.

He made the picture smooth and even across the cotton. They looked like a family and a team.

The first part is beauty, which seems easy but is actually more stressful than talent. With talent you can rely on costumes or props or something else entirely. With beauty, it's all on these little girls to appear poised, to have personalities.

Jewel hits all her marks, but her smile seems put on, too toothy, if that's possible. Pink seems to have fallen out of favour, and gowns are in blues, greens, aqua tones. Everyone looks like they're floating under water.

Sashay comes out in her shimmery sky blue and nails every move. Even though it seemed like she didn't pay attention during Rhonda's training sessions, she picked up all the important things. Turns, positions, head tilt. As she waves, the crowd gives loud applause and cheers. The judges smile and nod at each other.

"She could win. She could win big."

"Sashay is a winner. Our winner. That's a lot of money fanned around that trophy, Linda."

"It's not about the money."

"Well, it's nice, honey. It'd be real nice."

They hold hands and sit in their seats to watch the rest of the girls parade across the stage. Before Linda goes to help Sashay get into her talent costume and prep her, Kevin holds her tightly, strokes her back and hair.

"Next time we should stay in a hotel," Kevin says.

During her talent portion, Sashay juts her hip out when the music starts and doesn't stop giving her all. Foot taps, booty swirl, kicks, shimmy, shimmy, shimmy, body roll, shake. She blows kisses that could knock out a tall building. But then she goes too big with her windmills and jumps, and her hair starts to come undone. Blonde curls hurtle from her head onto the stage, an errant tendril hits the judge's table, her wig flying off, pieces of her stripped, broken in front of everyone.

The murmurs from the crowd turn into muffled laughs and tsks. Some stop looking because it's too humiliating. Others fire up their cameras. The judges, so taken with her earlier, are scratching at their scorecards. Linda can't see their faces but knows they're not smiling now. Kevin squeezes Linda's hand, a different pressure from earlier, a solid, heart-thudding urgency. Sashay performed perfectly, but it doesn't matter. All the girls have big hair, sparkles, eyes wide open like dolls. Her daughter does and doesn't look like the others. Underneath her spray tan is her real skin, peachy with mosquito bite marks. Linda's drugstore mascara is supposed to be waterproof, but charcoal streaks through layers of foundation.

Sashay doesn't stop dancing, stomps the fallen hair as she goes into her grand finishing move, a spin and half flip. She doesn't realize the damage is done, that her hair looks like it's been attacked by a feral cat, what's left unadorned with sparkle. Hands thrown in the air, she smiles so big that the flipper pops out for a second before she reins it in with her tongue.

Under the "I"

Outside the front doors of the Elks Hall, women jostle to light up. The clink of brooches and pins heard as coats collide, as they wrestle to get under the awning, the best spot to smoke and complain. They hold Craven As like daggers, ready to fight. In the dim neon of the "Bingo" sign, the tops of their heads glow, a glisten in their perms. Wind whips falling snow into their cluster and they start back inside, ready to savour refills of burnt coffee and fountain pop. Shirley butts out, watches her younger sister, Mary Beth, rush for the doors, her lavender polyester pants crinkling against her Depends.

Shirley's station is decorated with fresh cards, the used ones folded into squares and stacked to her left. Her cards all touch each other in an even layout. No mismatched edges, all colour coded, numbered, in order. Unlike Mary Beth's area, hers has nothing extraneous, no charms, no insipid dolls, no heart-framed family. Shirley rounds the shoulders of her coat over the back of a folding chair. Coffee steams in Styrofoam to her right.

"Your cards are on my side," Mary Beth says.

"They're perfectly organized," says Shirley.

Mary Beth sticks out her elbow to show the cards' infringement on her space. Grinding her teeth, Shirley sets up again, moves everything to please her sister, stamps each card down with just enough force to shake the table a little. Mary Beth furrows her brow.

"Our table needs a win," Shirley says.

"I need a win," Mary Beth says.

"Pish," says Shirley.

As children, they would fight like this. No pinches under the dinner table or swats on the way to church. They would bicker, unlike sisters, more like an old married couple in a struggle for power. Their relationship a familiar blend of connection and conflict. Mary Beth played volleyball and Shirley played basketball, games different enough to make competition more interesting when they compared points and team esteem and parental attendance, especially if they both played the same night. Debates over physical prowess were more complicated.

As they got older, they never fought over boyfriends, only over whose was better, more attractive, more likely to become a manager at the smelter instead of a lowly labourer. Mary Beth hated for Shirley to hold back information, preferred a kiss and tell, and she always knew when she wasn't getting enough gossip by the nervous way Shirley would rap her fingers on the back of her other hand. Their late night teenaged conversations across their bedroom would culminate in smoking, their new shared pastime. They would puff and shush each other, huddled together at their open bedroom window.

Now, in their seventies, they squabble over pot roasts and pound cake precision, the merits of supermarket mystery novels and bingo, the one activity that levels the playing field.

Someone could win at bingo, a win measured in dollars. It's all up to chance.

Last year, Mary Beth's Arnie died. Shirley's Frank is still holding on, a millwright who retired early. He watches television crime dramas while she's out and falls asleep in the armchair before the killer is revealed. When she wakes him up, he spurts and shouts that he knows who did what. Sometimes he accuses her, then zonks right back out, and Shirley leaves him there. On those nights, the bed is hers. She stretches in all directions, can dream. Frank in bed next to her isn't uncomfortable, but he gets in the way.

The bulky snack cart lurches around the room, two perky uniformed volleyball players needed to propel it from one table to the next. Chips jiggle on metal clips, individually wrapped Rice Krispies treats stacked high below them; the coffee urn gleams between their doughy girl faces. Shirley watches the young athletes struggle to turn the cart around a corner, wonders if their thin arms could even spike a ball. Shirley hands a loonie to the girl wearing her warm-up jacket around her waist, pours her own coffee.

All the women at their table have their own rituals. Mary Beth has her full display of junk, like that stuffed gorilla the size of her head. Annie mutters to herself with each jittery spat of her dauber. Janine alternates as she dabs, pink then green then purple then pink again. Pauline likes to be precise, but her eyes are bad, and she refuses to wear her bifocals. Her card is always a Rorschach mess. Shirley takes another sip of dark coffee, scalding caffeine her ritual, the heat already seeping out of it.

The caller repeats himself, and everyone giggles. He's so young, not quite fifty, wears jeans. Everyone says he reminds them of someone else. Son, nephew, that boy from down the lane with the cowlick. He calls the letter in a low voice, then bellows the number. Mary Beth touches one of her photos. In the corner of her eye Shirley sees this, knows her sister is looking for a stroke of luck.

Forty years ago, the two of them had worked the afternoon shift together in the hospital kitchen, would commiserate over their husbands' complaints of late dinners and children unable to complete their homework. Mary Beth got Shirley the job when there was an open spot to fill after a girl got knocked up by a surgeon. To feed and clean for money felt special and irritating in an important way, new emotions that waved over Shirley like fragrant soap.

They worked well together, had a system. Rigged the deep fryer to hold more frozen fries, baked the cheese sandwiches instead of frying to leave time for smoke and gossip breaks. They shared inside jokes in the walk-in freezer.

After three years together at the sinks, at the cutting boards, Shirley had to quit to stay home with her son, who got drunk and walked into a moving car. Her son spent most of his time reading comic books and ignoring her when she asked him what he wanted for lunch. Figuring that without a job she had free time, Mary Beth asked Shirley to pop over and feed her family too.

"You've got time. The girls are big enough now to set the table. And with you gone, I've got to pick up the slack at work," Mary Beth had said.

And Shirley did it, day after day, cooked for two families, wasn't thanked twice as much. Every square inch of her son was bandaged for months, and once he was mostly healed and she had forgiven most of him for being an idiot, she decided, with much encouragement from Frank, not to go back to work. She continued to cook for Mary Beth, still up at the hospital perfecting skins on puddings. She fed Mary Beth's husband, a manager at the smelter, and their young daughters, then ran home to her own family. Sometimes she burnt the roast in her own oven, but she never set off the smoke alarm at her sister's.

"Bingo," hollers Annie.

It's a small pot, only forty-two dollars. They all sigh. Shirley recaps her green dauber. Mary Beth looks at her, whines with her eyes. The two of them haven't had a bingo in weeks, although Mary Beth shouldn't complain. A month ago she got two bingos in one night, and one was on a double pay card, so she had enough money to treat everyone for breakfast the next day at the Zellers restaurant, which they sometimes do, but she didn't. Spent it on a fancy As-Seen-On-TV Ultra-Mop, which she talks about as much as possible.

Those afternoons at Mary Beth's house had been easy. The girls had piano or dance lessons until at least five o'clock. Arnie walked in the door at a quarter past four and was never a nuisance in the kitchen. By the time he'd put his coat in the closet, hung his hat on the hook, dropped his shoes on the mat, and unbuttoned his cuffs, dinner would be in the oven. Arnie would ask about her day and tell her that her housedress was flattering. He smiled with his eyes and had one dimple. She'd put the kettle on. Standing at her side, he would reach up high to get the good tea from the top shelf, curl an arm around her waist to sneak past her in the narrow space between the stove and table. One touch, one motion swayed into another. Their bodies came together in the hallway or alcove. Arnie was firm but generous, and his breath tasted of wedding almonds.

The table set with dinnerware and a meal, Shirley would be satisfied, dressed, out of the house before the girls were back. Back at home, Frank never noticed her flushed cheeks as she whisked through the kitchen, still didn't ask how her day was, and at night he grunted the same old way in their bedroom twice a week. He did comment on her new habit of whistling as she prepared supper. He liked it, and that made Shirley happy.

Someone at their table needs to win big. They could use a little fun. Shirley would love some fun, a morning out with the ladies, sniping and cackling at each other. The caller repeats himself, and Mary Beth shuffles. She examines her cards, covers them with her arms as though it's a test she wants everyone else to fail.

"I think this card's lucky," Mary Beth says.

"Maybe," Shirley says.

After the girls left for college, Mary Beth quit the hospital, and Shirley had to quit her afternoon visits to her sister's house. The first childfree weekend, Shirley invited her sister and Arnie to dinner. Over beef and potatoes, the two couples smoked their way through talk of who had the more capable children, whose relationship yielded the more ridiculous arguments, whose wedding photos held up to the test of time. Mary Beth hated the bridesmaid's dress she'd had to wear to Shirley's wedding and used it as a stone to throw at the whole ceremony. Shirley always felt the dress was flattering, that in fact Mary Beth had looked better, more radiant than she did in her ivory gown.

Their husbands escaped to watch hockey in the next room. A relief for Shirley. She hadn't looked anyone in the eye all evening, kept her attention on the meal. Had carefully planned multiple courses, excuses to get up from the table. Shirley and Mary Beth picked at the leftover tomatoes from the salad. In the living room, Frank threw an ashtray at the wall. Mary Beth flinched. The wrong person must have scored.

"Well, I know you agree. I got the better husband," Mary Beth said.

Shirley poured two cups of coffee, and they sat and smoked and sipped. They stared at each other, then Mary Beth's eyes changed focus, cast down on Shirley's fingers as they slapped at the skin of her other hand.

"It's not a contest," said Shirley.

"You prefer Arnie. Of course you do. Frank's crass. No offence," Mary Beth said, then blew a stream of smoke into her sister's face.

"I'm not offended."

"I know."

Mary Beth added more sugar, more milk until her coffee looked beige. Shirley listened to the clink of the spoon in the cup, the men's conversation in the next room, her own throat swallowing saliva. Arnie broke off talk of a penalty to go to the bathroom. Shirley finished her coffee and walked out of the kitchen.

She found Arnie in the bathroom, knew he'd been waiting for her, waiting for a moment. She'd liked the way he'd combed his hair, swept to the side. He closed the door, pressed her back against the glass shower door. They kissed in a fury, sucked at the pulse of each other before she moved away. Hands clasped with Arnie's, she sat on the toilet seat, wet with a dribble of Frank's pee. Frank, too lazy to lift the seat. Frank yelled for Arnie to check out the shit those asshole referees think they're pulling. She opened the bathroom door and pushed Arnie away. Their skin slowly lost contact, until only the tips of their fingers touched for a few final seconds of electricity.

After that, instead of afternoons with Shirley, Arnie spent them with rye on the rocks. For the rest of his life. Shirley took up badminton, and Mary Beth joined her even though she suffered from tendonitis, strain from hauling steamer trays. They played three times a week. Shirley let Mary Beth win some of the time. The loser had to buy the winner coffee and a muffin after the game. They lingered at the coffee shop and never compared husbands again.

Across the room, the Botanical Society table celebrates another win. Shirley huffs, scouts the room for those volleyball players and their charcoal coffee. When she gets home she can stay up late, long after Frank's gone to sleep, sip rye and play solitaire, compete against herself, her own personal cycle of win–lose.

A year ago, Arnie fell all the way to the bottom of the hill from the pub to the lip of the river. Died taking a leak, pants splayed, Y fronts open, wet and pickled. On her walk home from her book club, Shirley found him. In the spring snow, she bent to him, brushed soggy flakes from his face, took a last fond look at him before she zipped him up, walked over to the police station, and called his wife. That night, Mary Beth couldn't find her glasses, so Shirley drove over, picked her up, sat in silence while Mary Beth complained that she had to change out of her pyjamas just to look at Arnie's dead body.

"No luck. I was wrong," Mary Beth says.

"You deserve a win. Maybe Wednesday," Shirley says.

Annie's meagre bingo is their only win of the night, and they let her off the hook. No breakfast tomorrow. Mary Beth takes her time collecting her charms; her cramped, sore hands make it difficult to pack her duffle bag neatly. Shirley helps put away everything except the photographs. One of her sister's grandchildren, one of Arnie. After she's stowed everything away, Shirley takes Mary Beth's hand. They sit like this, ready to go but not ready yet, hands together.

At the end of the night everyone is at their slowest as they reclaim belongings, fasten coats, knot scarves. Outside they stand together, smoke one last one before heading home. Shirley and Mary Beth stand side by side. They exhale old breath, then smoke, then breath, and more smoke until the subtleties of grey subside, and they stamp out their cigarettes, their wordless goodbye.

Cold Cuts

"Pass me the obituaries," I say to Mark, holding out my hand. His curly head is buried in the paper. It gets delivered in the afternoon, but he likes to read it the next morning while he waits for his on-call call. He's always going over yesterday's news while he waits for work to let him know he can work. I haven't had a job since I got fired from the printing place for photocopying my boobs. I'd worked there only six months, and paper was obviously not my niche.

"There is no separate section for obituaries."

I keep my hand extended until he relents and slaps the paper into my hand. I'm looking for funerals to attend. Good ones, with lots of extra food to bring home. It's good to have a purpose, one that isn't sitting around here pretending I'm good at domestic shit.

"The Rossis are having one on Saturday," I yell, because I like to be loud in the morning to wake myself up, and it keeps Mark on his toes.

"Which Rossis?"

Mark's hunched over the kitchen table eating a green-wrapped mandarin orange. As he chews a segment, he presses the crinkles out of the paper with his index fingers. When he gets up for a glass of water, I crumple it into a ball and throw it at him.

"The ones up the street. Four blocks away. By the park. It's the closest one." There are so many old people in this small town, and they're dropping like flies, so I've decided to go about this the easy route and pick the funeral within walking distance. Mark's car is a piece of shit. We need to keep ourselves fed, and I'm a go-getter, but no one around seems to want to acknowledge that.

"Nat, are you really going to do this?" Mark picks up the ball of green paper and smooths it out on the counter.

"No, *we* are going to. It's a good idea. My idea. I'm writing it on your calendar. Don't be such a pussy."

The first time I crashed here, I made fun of Mark's calendar. His mom gave it to him. She'd gotten it free from some insurance company, and each month has a photograph of a different old man and his old car. I'm only supposed to have seen three months' worth of polished steel and commemorative car show hats because Mark says it's bad luck to flip ahead. He pins the bottom of the calendar down. The morning after that first night, I wrote "Mark sucks!" in one square of each month. The calendar hangs right above the shoe rack by the door, an unfriendly greeting from unattractive, old losers. Thank fuck, Mark hasn't posed with his crappy car for some small town insurance promo.

"I went to school with his granddaughter, so it's not like we don't know the Rossis. And that old guy used to yell at us to get off of his lawn, or he'd knock our 'bony asses into the river, goddamn it!' Oh, memories. And now he's gone."

Mark pulls the curtains open, and the kitchen fills with light, revealing sticky rings on the counter. He pulls out a fresh sponge and wipes the surface clean.

"We used to play on the other side of the river," he says.

Mark throws the sponge into the sink and comes back to finish his orange. I grab the last piece before he gets to it.

"Which is the wrong side of the river?" I ask.

Mark frowns at me and puts his hands in his pockets. "Whatever side you're on, Nat."

I hold the orange slice up to his mouth, and he hesitates before opening. I pop it in gently, and he bites down, satisfied. I can only fuck with him so much, but he needs me around to shake things up.

I thought Mark was a creep because he never tried anything with me. No gawking when Amy and I made out at a bush party. Never felt his hand climb up under my skirt. He didn't pin me to the side of his car, his dick ready-aim-fire in his pants. Mark was the guy at the party holding an always half-empty beer, slotted in the corner while everyone else did the talking and the dancing and the living. He was just there. I didn't understand why people invited him everywhere. He just took up space.

Four months ago he held back my hair while I puked my guts out. A chunk of sausage landed on his pant leg, but he didn't care, just told me to stop apologizing. Amy left me in a hallway after she convinced me we could each shotgun a two-litre of cider. When I asked someone where the bathroom was,

Mark opened the door, and I crawled in. He didn't wipe the strings of saliva and booze from my mouth either. I liked that.

After the puke incident I looked closer. He was still in the corner, but he laughed. He spilled his beer. I even saw him adjust his package once. That made it all right to talk to him a few weeks later.

"Hi. Mark, right?"

"Yeah. Hi."

He was deep into some NHL conversation with Jer, some idiot who wanted to take naked pictures of me last year. When he asked, I had my period, so I told him and he didn't think that was very sexy. Later I found out that Jer took naked pictures of himself instead. He's a douchebag.

"Hey, Nat, I've got an itchy sack. Could you shave it for me? I've got ..." Jer rooted around in his pocket as if any of this was funny, "about a dollar thirty and some fifty–fifty tickets from last week's game. You in?"

Mark started to walk away, but I grabbed his arm, then kicked Jer in the shin before he headed into the living room.

"I'm only on my first drink of the night," I said, gripping Mark's arm.

"Mark, the game starts in ten," the douchebag yelled.

"Okay. I'll be there."

I cut to the chase so Mark could watch hockey and I could go smoke. "Good job with the hair holding. That's usually a girl's job, but you knew what you were doing." I patted him on the back as if he'd scored the first goal of the game.

"Don't worry about it. The puke on my pants was thanks enough." He tapped me on the shoulder, a beer firmly in his hand. It was all over my sweater before I could pull away.

"I got beer on you. Sorry."

I took off my sweater and threw it on a chair. My shoulder glistened with drops of beer. Mark pulled his sleeve over his fist and wiped them away.

"*Mark. Game's on.*"

Jer never shut up.

"Thanks again. See you later? Second floor bathroom? Eleven-thirty? I need to finish this up early tonight. Better to puke before midnight." I stroked my hand along his sweater and gripped his fingers. My nails dug in just enough. He looked me in the eye before I let go and headed out to the porch.

From the kitchen I saw him watching me during the third period. We met in the bathroom at eleven-thirty. We kissed for a while, his tongue weak, fighting a losing battle against mine. He remembered my sweater smelling of beer and offered to drive me home in his ugly car. I pushed him out onto the street while he tried to unlock the passenger side door. Then he dropped me off at my parents' house. All night he watched me from the other room, he stalked me, and he kissed me. When I tried to undo his pants on the way home, he grabbed hold of my hand and set it underneath his on the stick shift, our fingers curled together.

A tray stacked with deli meats is set precariously close to the edge of the counter. Some careless mourner must have unloaded it too quickly, telling a nostalgic story, and crying. I'll keep my fond "kids being thrown in the river" memory to myself.

Mark is impressive. He was made for funerals, so quiet, solemn, respectful. A real suckhole. He sits in a high-backed chair and listens to ladies talk about card night.

Mark doesn't know it yet, but I could be an entrepreneur. I'm working the room. I am making a difference. I am being productive. I hug old women; I deposit their used tissues in the garbage; I help carry platters of cheese to the table and bowls of olive pits into the kitchen. This is a lot more work than I did at my last job. Consoling people in shifts, doling out looks of deep understanding, touching wet lipstick- and antipasto-stained napkins. Only once at my old job did a woman sob in my presence and that was because three boxes of legal paper fell on her foot.

"Old Mr. Rossi. All us kids in the neighbourhood knew him. What a joker." I repeat this line as I make the rounds.

No one eats the buns and cold cuts and cheese. They're all separate, so everyone has to make their own sandwich. When my grandmother died a few months ago, there was way more food. Way more options. She always liked to take care of us all and set aside money to make sure her funeral was full-on catered with hot items, things you could make a meal out of. This spread is fine but not spectacular. Better for carting home, I guess. I have no problem slapping some pre-cut items together, being resourceful.

Mrs. Rossi is working harder than anyone. When someone

gets up off the couch, she plumps each brown floral cushion until it looks as though no one had been sitting there at all. That's how it will look tomorrow when she wakes up alone.

"I know Stephanie. We went to high school together," I tell a man in a short-sleeved shirt who doesn't speak much English.

Mark doesn't remember what Stephanie looked like, even though she was always in front of a microphone at assemblies talking about charity phone book deliveries and cake walks and animal rescues.

I almost dump a full bowl of mixed olives onto a girl in black velvet as she steps out of the bathroom. Stephanie. In the seven months since graduation, I'd forgotten how large her hips were. Made for babies and backdoor lovin' is what we used to say.

"Stephanie?"

"Yes."

She seems distracted. When my grandmother died, I grumbled and acted uncivilized. At least that's what my mother said. I didn't even eat any of that food, just stared at it from the bathroom door. Foolish. The heels of Stephanie's shoes dig holes into the carpet. Mourners walk hard.

"It's Natalie."

"I know."

"Sorry. Hope you're holding up."

"Thanks. I am. I'm okay."

I try to wave Mark over. The woman next to him can't let him go. He's opening her childproof pill bottles and handing her each dose. He is supposed to be here for me, be my assistant. Stephanie smiles at the room, her eyes unfocused. She's not looking at anyone.

"I heard your grandmother died recently. Sorry to you, too. I was away at school then, I didn't ..."

"Yeah. There is so much food here."

I hold up my bowl of olives.

"Thanks for helping."

She doesn't need to say it. She thinks I'm here because I know how hard it is to lose a grandparent. No sense telling her she's wrong. Her lip quivers a bit, and she looks deeply into the olive bowl. I put the olives on a side table, reach out, and pull her in close for a hug. Stephanie falls against me, and I feel her shake. It only lasts a moment, and then she's composed again, her face screwed up as though she's remembering hard.

"Mark!" I say.

I yank Stephanie along as I make my way to the dining room. It's time to pack up. Mark stands beside the table of food, a highball glass filled with wine in his hands. The pill-bottle woman has left and most people are embracing Mrs. Rossi and getting the hell out of there. The sun is almost down, just a thin layer of red visible in the sky. It'll be snowing by dinnertime.

"Mark, remember Stephanie? Stephanie, Mark."

Mark puts his arm over her shoulders and looks down at her with sincerity. Stephanie melts into his chest and heaves her shoulders. Mark walks her over to the couch. He's unbelievable.

Empty, cheap plastic containers bulge in my purse. While

Stephanie breaks down on Mark, I pull out the containers. I walk around the table loading up while everyone else dabs their eyes and thinks about the next time they'll all have to sit around like this, in someone else's house, some other old dead person buried and gone and mourned with a plate of salami, roasted red pepper stains on their clothes. On the way out, I shoot the guns at Stephanie and mouth that I'll call her.

"That was harder than manual labour." My purse smells like a day-old sandwich.

Flakes as big as my fist fall around us. Mark takes my hand and walks me down the steep embankment.

"You made out well," he says and taps my bag. I dig my heels into the snow and make him pull me. As soon as we're on level ground, I let go and run ahead, kicking fresh powder at him. He doesn't try to catch up.

I thought Mark was a bit off because he said it didn't matter that I didn't have a job. He thought I'd figure this all out; being young and from a broken home, I'd need extra time to find out where I should be. I punched him in the arm three times for judging me. So, I have a dad who skipped town and a bitchy mom who hated him and parts of me for being parts of him. I couldn't even believe Mark would use those stupid words right in from of me. Broken. When I thought about it later, he seemed pretty fucking wise for an on-call carpenter's assistant. I wasn't sure I could trust him. When my mother told me to get another job or get out, I pounded the pavement for three days with my resumé printed on stolen paper. This garbage town didn't get me. If I couldn't get job interviews, I'd figure things out myself. So I called Mark to come haul my stuff over in his shitty car on the fourth day.

Mark works for two weeks straight and makes enough for two months' rent. I'm getting ready for my funeral, which he says isn't necessary.

"It's important to me, Mark. Don't be such a selfish dick."

I need him to soothe their pain, be my soft-spoken working man, the boring, normal distraction. The dead guy was pretty rich, and the food will be heaped on the table, but lately Mark's been buying groceries and thinks we should use them. I told him I don't want to cook food I haven't earned. He refuses to put on the khakis I've ironed, even though this is the first time I've ironed his clothes.

"I want to stay home today. Just watch the game."

There's a six-pack of beer in the fridge but no cider, which is what I've been drinking lately. I drank the rest of it last night. He only bought what *he* wanted this time. I haven't figured out how to convince old ladies and their overbearing children to fork over their leftover booze.

There's a lot more laughing at these gatherings than I thought there'd be; families remember the most ridiculous parts of a life. Last week, at Jerry DePaolo's celebration of life, someone had brought up the school musical from 1963, when Jerry had tumbled through the plywood backdrop, but still managed to sing the song with a concussion. The entire house had broken into the "Modern Major-General" song from *The Pirates of Penzance*. Dancing and pretending they had head injuries, the group swept me up, and I bobbed my head as if I knew the song, the words, the whole story. Some middle-aged sad sack told me about the song and the musical for thirty minutes after that.

We haven't been to a party in over a month, but we've been to six funerals. Mark didn't like when I convinced him to go to two in one day, but I say, "Get while the getting is good." He held the widow's hand at both funerals while I organized cold meatloaf into Ziploc freezer bags.

"Nat."

"What?"

"We have a fridge full of food here. You don't have to go funeral foraging."

"I want to!"

"Why? The food I bought will go bad if we don't eat it. Why do you need to go?"

The house where they're gathering is behind the nearby school playground. I used to play in the sandbox there, when I was a kid. You could see right into the front window while digging to nowhere with a plastic shovel. The family there was a lot older than mine, but they always had parties that spilled onto the front lawn. Everyone having a great time, saying cheers, and getting into sports arguments that didn't end in fist fights or smashed bottles.

Mark strokes my crossed arms. Those widows are vulnerable, but not me. Swipes of his rough palms on my skin aren't going to make me any less angry. He's left his half-empty beer on the table, and I try to kick it over. I miss.

"Nat. Please? There is no reason to go."

"I ironed your pants."

"And they look great. I can still wear them."

"Just sit around the house and wear khakis instead of sweatpants? What are you?"

"I'm not going."

His hands are still on me, and he's too good at maintaining eye contact, so I look away first. I kick at the table one more time, get the corner, and the bottle wobbles.

"Just one day off? I worked hard all week. And you know I hate fighting. Please. When do I say no? Why are you pushing this?"

Mark kisses my cheek and rests his head beside mine. He's freshly shaven and smells shower clean, and I think of formaldehyde and mothballs.

"Quit interrogating me. I'm going. I can do shit on my own."

I break away and head over to the bedroom. I strip out of my sweatshirt and stand in my bra and panties and press the steaming iron over my only black pants, my Saturday mourning pants that make my ass look good even when it shouldn't.

Jer told me that Mark had never had a steady girlfriend before me.

"He's probably a fucking virgin. Why would he want a slut like you? You're more my style."

Jer was wrong. About two things. Mark had a steady girl-friend, Jenny Parker, in grade six. And he'd fucked a girl on a hockey trip and another one that he'd dated for a month before she dumped him because he drove a truck with a canopy. She was embarrassed to have sex with someone with a canopy. He sold the truck to some hunter and bought the crappy car. I wouldn't have minded the canopy. I don't really mind the crap-py car. Don't even mind fucking in it. Mark likes to do it in the bedroom, in a bed.

It's snowing hard, but I put on spike-heeled boots. Mark told me to take his car, but I don't want to drive in the snow. Or owe him anything. I've never driven his car before. He's en-joying himself, sitting in front of the television as the afternoon turns into darkness too quickly. I hear goodbye when I storm out the door. Probably happy I didn't make a mess of his beer. Tiny flakes make a veil in front of me as I walk. I slow down, watch my pin-heeled feet to make sure they don't slip.

I thought Mark was abnormal because he didn't know how to yell. His voice is soothing, low, and sometimes I don't quite catch what he says. I yell out that I can't hear him, that he should speak up. This makes him laugh. He doesn't take my anger seriously. Which makes me seriously furious.

I thought he was abnormal because he refused to make ob-scene comments about me to his friends. Because he wasn't like Jer and their bro gang. I told them about our sex life, bragged about it for him. I thought Mark wasn't ready for me because he sometimes stuttered when I came into the room. I thought Mark was horny just because he'd kiss me goodnight.

A car swerves at me, and I jump into the snowbank. I didn't see anything coming at me, only the wild flakes and the tips of my boots as I watched myself shuffle down the middle of the street. No snowplows have come through yet, and it's been coming down heavy for hours. Snow up past my shins, I stand in the cold, realize my purse has fallen somewhere in this whiteout.

The car's going fast, a shiny black rush in the snow. The hill is long, and whoever is driving pumps the brakes and manages to slow down before the park, drive smoothly for a few metres. Then the car catches ice. The driver does everything right. Tries to turn into the skid, but the car hits something in the bank, and the whole thing flips, then flips two more times, and rests near the snow-blanketed teeter-totters.

The crash is quiet, snow muffling the sound of the impact. I stare at the car's tires, the bottom of the vehicle facing up, collecting snow now too. I pull myself out of the bank and find my purse on the other side of the road. I hadn't zipped it up, and things are missing. I salvage my wallet and some lip gloss, but my keys are gone.

I run to the car, slipping and sliding down the hill. It looks cradled in a white sheet. My heels stick into the snow, and it feels like I've been walking for hours when I get to the car. I reach for the door, stumble. I take a step back to steady myself and lose one of my boots in the snow, pulling out a socked foot. I trip trying to find the boot and land against the driver's side window. When I look in, I can just see her white hair through the window. I brush snow away with my glove and see a veiny head hang limp from her jowls, not even a neck anymore. She doesn't move or whimper, but I see a strand of smoky breath filter out of her mouth.

Sometimes old people still drive. They make their way to friends' houses or even go visit other old people clogging up hospital rooms. The hospital is in a good location. They get a nice view in those last moments, snow coming down onto the mountains, landing gently on the roofs of houses in the valley. My view is the wall of the house next door and the alley full of Christmas trees.

I try the door, pull on the handle, but it's locked. The driver's side window is shattered but still intact. I push on the glass, puncture a hole just big enough to push a finger in. If I try to smash through the brittle mess, I'll cut her hand, which dangles right there. Might even slash her face.

She'd turned from the top of the hill on her way somewhere, and then, there I was walking right in the middle of the goddamn road thinking about whose pants I iron. I want to blame Mark for this, but he wasn't in the road. He's at home, warm and nice and drinking at a responsible pace. Mark had washed the sheets this morning, because after drinking all that cider I'd been too lazy to get out of bed to puke. Mark always walked on the sidewalk, even if it was covered in snow. She'd cranked the wheel to miss me. And now I'm not mowed down, bloodying that snowbank. I only lost my keys.

I watch for more breath. My fingers still slotted through the glass, I grab her hand. It's freezing cold. I crouch in the snow and hold her fingers until I see another weak stream of air come out of her mouth.

I haul myself out of the bank, pull my boot over my snow-clotted sock. The funeral is around the corner. I run through the drifts, boot full of snow crunching and melting through my sock. At the end of the block, I turn back to see the car, already turned almost white by snow, her gloveless hand and jowls invisible to me. I take a turn, climb up another hill.

At the hospital, I tell some lady in pink teddy bear scrubs about the accident. She tells me to calm down, and I tell her I am calm and that she should calm down but also that this is serious. Hospital workers scuffle around behind a glass partition. A nurse says that someone is already on their way down and that I can wait.

I leave and walk down the hill on the other sidewalk, which somehow has been sanded. When I get to the bottom, I watch paramedics pull the driver from the car, pile blankets around her on the stretcher. A few neighbours stand around too. Some look out from their front windows. I don't know if she's dead or not.

After the ambulance is gone, I walk a few blocks, sit on the steps under the covered green staircase that leads home.

I wait until I think the funeral will have ended and someone else will have taken the canapés into the kitchen. I wait a little while after that, just to be sure.

When I walk in the door, Mark's wearing his khaki pants. I can see them on his legs, propped up on his old ottoman. He's got a half-full beer in his hand, the game on quietly, as if he's mourning something. The click of the door startles him, and he jerks around to see what's happening as I shake snow from my coat.

"Sorry," I say as I strip off my wet clothes, drop my boots on the rubber mat underneath the calendar.

"How was it?"

I go sit on the couch beside him, reach over and take a sip of his beer.

"It was shit. There'll be better ones," I say, my voice barely raised.

Particleboard Man

Hey, you've reached Ryan and Cindy. Can't take your call, but don't worry, we'll get back to you real soon.

There's no real good reason to keep the message, but she can't think of a good reason to erase it either. Cindy tells herself she'll wait until the tape snaps, and it'll be gone for good. Strong as steel that tape, over ten years on record, eleven and a half months since he's been gone. She doesn't get a lot of calls, just from her mother, her friend Heather, who's almost always on night shift, the dentist. Mostly she listens to Ryan in the early evening. When she feels like muting *Wheel of Fortune*, clicking play to hear the purr of "real soon" or the curt, hard "can't take your call." She remembers the way he'd clicked the record button, his wrist at a ninety degree angle, his elbow resting on the wicker placemat under the phone, the bowl of keys beside the answering machine.

Cindy clamps her hand around her whisky fizz and thinks about all the things she's neglected to do in her rush to make it to the bar: wash her work clothes, let the cat out, set up her voice mail, throw out that piece of shit answering machine. The old, heavy machine somehow still works after twenty years of loyal service. Ryan's voice coos through the message whenever anyone calls and she can't get to the phone in time.

Two nights ago, Heather came with wine and Chinese food. They didn't even talk about Ryan. Heather was worried about her dad's surgery the next morning and her son's new girlfriend. Cindy told a story about a man she'd seen driving a car with two pigs strapped in seatbelts in the back seat. They snorted and laughed, made pigs' faces. But after a bottle and a half, they moved from the kitchen into the living room. Cindy stared hard at the answering machine, and Heather ran over and forced Cindy's hand over the delete button.

"No!" Cindy shouted and grabbed at Heather's wrist. The two of them wrestled above the particleboard table, the cordless phone and answering machine rattling as their knees knocked against the thin faux wood legs.

"You've got to let go! This is old!"

Heather pinches Cindy's neck. Cindy yelps and whips her arms, tangled with Heather's behind her. They break free, and Cindy clutches the answering machine in her arms. Heather is slumped on the arm of the couch. Both breathe heavily.

"I'm not ready."

"Okay," Heather said, "but I'm ready to help you rip off that Band-Aid when it's time. Should we drink some more wine?"

"Of course," Cindy said.

Ryan and Cindy. The message lies to the people who call. At thirty-eight, she's only been with one man, and now he's just a voice, two sentences held in outdated technology. His voice used to mean that she was useful. Asking where his underwear has gotten to, what time he has to be at the doctor's office, which drawer has the bottle opener. Cindy, wordless, would find the underwear, or hand him the doctor's reminder card, or open his beer for him. At night she could get him to brush his teeth with a smile, could steer him to bed with one hand on his shoulder. Even sex was seamless, though not so quiet. The one time she would let her vocal cords loose. At least, for the first few years that's how it was. Then her silence became as annoying as a jackhammer is to someone not wearing protective ear-gear. At least, that's pretty much what he said to her.

The clink of beer bottles in the bar comforts her. People are around her. Lots of people. Young men. The sort of people who might talk to her. Maybe not tonight. But one day. But hopefully tonight. After they'd invited her over to a quiet corner table, she could tell them about the busted-up dirt bike in her garage and the whirlpool bath she'd had installed. As long as it wasn't Travis Smith, from Smith and Son's Sunshine Pool & Spa, because he already knew about the bath and didn't seem very interested in the dirt bike as he wheeled the dolly past Cindy in her neon and orange vest and steel toes. These people will be interested in her, want to know what she's about. She's been in every Thursday, just once a week for three weeks. No need to seem like a drunk.

Construction workers shoot pool in the corner, and a group of guys sit at a round table with two pitchers of beer, talking and sometimes pointing at the TV. Cindy watches the activity in the room in the reflection of Budweiser and Pilsner and Kokanee mirrors hanging behind the bar. In her peripheral vision, she sees three paint-splattered guys trying to build a beeramid with their empty bottles. Adorable. But it doesn't matter how cute Cindy thinks they are; it's what they think of her that matters. Brown glass clatters and bottles roll. The paint-splattered guy with the long hair and the one with the shaved head pour their beer dregs onto their buddy who knocked over their hard work. In retaliation he pulls the ponytail of the long-haired guy. It all looks like so much fun. Vibrant, like what her co-workers must do after a shift together.

She'd been the younger woman with Ryan, but by just enough. That was then. It was all about then. When there was a then, there had been so much time, a future. Time, in the future, when she could make decisions and wait. But Ryan did not like waiting. Ryan said he wanted to be in the now. And that is why he had to leave. But to Cindy, that was their sameness. They both wanted to be in the now. She didn't want to think about what would happen in the future. She just wanted it to be there, somewhere away from her and Ryan and their wicker mat and velvety sofa and their Napoli pizza delivered to the door on Friday nights. Ryan, with his Canucks jersey and his 501s, and his hairy wrists protruding from the microwave popcorn while they watched every city's worth of *CSI* on tape.

He meant he wanted other things to happen in the now. That is why. They had a different idea of what should happen in the now they were both living in.

Though she didn't mark it on a calendar, Cindy knows the exact last moment Ryan looked at her with interest. It was the last time they had sex. He came into the kitchen, and she had spilled red wine on her shirt and had taken it off to toss into the washing machine. She was wearing just a bra and jeans, and he had come at her shoulder with his teeth like it was prime rib. While they were down on the kitchen floor, he looked into her eyes like it was the first thrill, and she was so grateful that she grabbed for a tea towel and wrapped it around his head to hold it in place and keep their eyes locked on each other forever. But it only lasted two minutes, and then it was over. That was six years ago.

His new girlfriend is sweet and a teller at the credit union, with a teal green sedan and a well-defined chin. Cindy's chin is on its way out. The new girlfriend was very helpful when Cindy needed to assess her RRSPs, that's for sure. And Cindy has quite a few years on this new girlfriend. Being five years younger than your man isn't much when he can easily get himself a nice fertile one who's fourteen years younger than you are and clearly better at math because she works in a bank and is essentially a financial professional. Maybe she thinks that the future is far away too. Maybe he's recorded his hard consonants on her answering machine. She probably has her own personal voice mail. Of course she does.

Adding up the age differences and subtracting how many years apart isn't the kind of number crunching Cindy is used to. On a regular day she counts cars instead of money, but mostly she stands in the hot sun or rain, reflective vest over her T-shirt and the jeans she wishes she could just throw away. Seated at the bar in a pink skirt and white sandals feels right, more who she is on the inside. Although Cindy shifts constantly, tugs at her skirt even more constantly. The jeans she should just throw away are a protective stone-washed shell and cover her problem areas in a way that a silk camisole tucked into this skirt never could.

The bald guy stands next to her at the bar. He smiles at her, not politely. Cindy thinks this might be a seductive pose, the face of a man who knows he needs a more experienced woman. She also knows that she will have to try harder to appear like the more experienced woman.

"You gotta get back out there. He can't be having all the fun. You deserve to jump on some young guy, really take a ride."

Heather doesn't know how long it's been. Cindy hasn't been able to confide in her about that part of it. She knows it's been a long time, that Cindy hasn't flexed certain muscles in a long time. She doesn't know the date, doesn't know that Cindy stays up at night and tries to imagine other men's naked bodies lying next to her in bed, but can't really picture their arms around her, the warmth of their skin, that they have genitals at all. When she closes her eyes they're young and faceless, wearing

T-shirts and plaid pyjama bottoms. Just like Ryan. He's even in her terribly uninteresting fantasies.

They sat on the couch with more wine, and Heather was quiet for a while.

"Sorry about the answering machine. I wouldn't just delete it, you know."

Heather hugged Cindy, a big hug. Their full glasses touched, and some of Cindy's wine splashed onto a tan throw pillow. She raced to get salt and OxiClean.

"I know. But you're right. I have to do something. I just can't tell if I'm ready. How can anyone tell? Especially after so long."

Cindy sprinkled salt over the surface of the setting red stain, pressed granules into the fabric. Cars drove by outside. In the dark, Cindy could see their lights zipping along the pavement, bright blips. People going home to loved ones, people finding their place.

"What about if we go out? You can look at guys, have some drinks, forget about that barfbag Ryan."

This isn't the first time Heather's suggested a night out, that they actually consume alcohol in public like they did when they were younger, when she met Ryan at a Little League fundraiser, and they held hands in the Lions Hall, and she felt her whole life warm up to the right temperature. Cindy has always turned her down. She already has to be in public for work all day long. Holding up a stop sign, waving people through. At night she wants to take a break from strangers, people. Heather is the only one she likes visiting with, at her place or here at home.

Heather pours more wine into Cindy's glass, empties the bottle into the wide bowl with a stem. They cackle about the man across from Heather who can't seem to get his house paint to match. When the wine is gone, Cindy looks down at her fluffy socks. The socks of someone who doesn't need to impress anyone. What would she wear?

"Okay. I'll go out. Tomorrow. I have the next day off."

"Really? You'll go out? Do you need me to be your wing woman?"

"Does that mean you serve me wings while I try and pick up men?"

"That would be a better use for the term. Do you want me there?"

Cindy turned Heather down. Her dad's surgery is in the morning. He'll be in recovery, and Heather needs to be there for her family. Her lazy brothers certainly won't be bringing food to her mom or ferrying her back and forth to the hospital. On her own is what Cindy needs if she's going to try and spend a night with another person. She's had enough practice lately spending nights alone in bed. That's why she's so out of practice touching another person.

"Babe, can I buy you a drink?" But this is not to her. The bald guy is talking to the bartender manning the taps in her black apron and grommet belt. The cotton of her Nickelback T-shirt so shoddy it will stretch in places and shrink in other places the first time it's thrown in the washing machine and dryer. But for now it's perfect, free of pills and snags, the plastic iron-on transfer still firmly rooted to the chintzy fibres. A woman should not think this way when she wants to get what the girl in the tight and shoddy concert tee could get. Maybe she should mention to the girl that she should wash in cold water and lay flat to dry.

The bartender huffs and fills a pint glass with foam, then grabs another, slides it under the spigot to collect the good beer. When she gives the full glass to the guy, Cindy realizes that they must already be a couple. She knows what he wants. He ignores her and walks back to the pool table, doesn't compliment her on the tightness of her jeans or ask when she gets off shift. He knows. He knows and doesn't care. She'll come home to him with her booze-scented clothes and overloaded key chain and wake him up in the middle of a dream about *Maxim*'s hottest female fighter pilots, and he'll grumble that she needs to make it up to him, and then she'll get her chance to ignore him, throw her shirt and jeans into the hamper to mingle with his sweaty clothes, and they'll go to sleep, backs facing each other.

"You've sucked that dry," the bartender says as she wipes the bar with a grey towel and grabs Cindy's empty glass from her hand. She's been slurping and clinking the ice cubes.

"Are you ready for another drink?"

The bartender holds up the glass, and Cindy bobs her head up and down. *Yes, another drink.* She could buy two for herself, just to get in the mood. Walk around the bar showing them off. In case anyone missed what she was drinking, now they would know, now they would see her taking her little sips and sitting quietly contemplating life and the problems with trying to live it. Someone would come up and set one in front of her when this was done and say, "This one's on me."

Her old melty ice cubes tumble out into the sink with a crash, and then the bartender is tossing new ones, cold and fresh, into a new glass and squirting the soda gun with indignation. The whisky comes down fast into the shot glass, and then Cindy is presented with a perfect new cocktail.

Cindy opens her mouth to thank the girl but is interrupted by the loud clang of a telephone. She retreats and clams up. The bartender reaches under the bar and pulls the receiver to her ear.

"Hello, Brat's Pub."

Cindy leans over and drinks through the straw, imagines that someone has to be watching her. Some man in this bar sees a woman alone drinking whisky. Cold, sugary booziness squirts into her mouth. She pulls back to admire the rosy lipstick ring left behind on the blue plastic. When she finishes this drink, she'll need to replenish a coat of Revlon Super Lustrous 440 Cherries in the Snow, but then, maybe the man who'd been watching her would think she was leaving and give up. His shyness would win and she would lose. She wonders which man is watching her. It's uncouth to turn around and search for him. She occasionally glances into the beer mirrors to check out if she is being checked out. But now that she's really thinking about it, she can feel his eyes on her. It is only a matter of time.

"Uh-huh. Five-fifty." The bartender covers the mouthpiece of the phone with her hand while she asks Cindy for payment. Cindy pushes three toonies across the bar.

"Keep the change." She gives the bartender her widest smile, eyebrows raised.

"Uh-huh. Yeah. Thanks." The bartender hangs up the phone, and Cindy isn't sure if she's the one being thanked or yeahed or uh-huhed.

Her bedside table is cluttered with magazines and biographies. Cindy had studied all the right older women: Goldie Hawn, Demi Moore. And locally too, she'd been paying attention: the woman who actually had a pool boy and had made love to him, the baker from across town who'd married her daughter's boyfriend. Her only concern was that so many of them seemed to have a rule about going without a bra. This was not something she had ever thought her breasts could handle. She disregarded this little amendment to her wardrobe, while taking the rest of her cues from them. She had also carefully thought to put a pair of slinky underwear into a Ziploc bag in her purse. When he took her home, she could excuse herself to freshen up, run her hand seductively along the hallway while making eye contact, and in the bathroom quickly change out of her Spanx and into the lacy ones before he'd change his mind about her.

The beeramid comes crashing down again. An empty Budweiser rolls across the floor and stops directly under her stool. The long-haired guy jogs over, beer stains mixed with the paint on his white coveralls. Cindy grips her whisky fizz and freezes. He bends over to retrieve the bottle but stumbles and grabs her thigh for support. Cindy clenches every muscle in her body and sucks at her drink. Using her leg to brace himself, he stands up, proudly holding the loose bottle. Cindy focuses on her almost empty drink and tries not to stare at him.

"Sorry." He brushes her leg as though he's dirtied it. Cindy smiles. He didn't call her lady or ma'am.

"Don't worry about it." Cindy looks over at him. It seems appropriate that after someone has groped and caressed a part of her body, even if it was for his own safety, she make eye contact. His eyes are green and dopey like a kitten's.

"Oh no. I got some on you there." He points at her lap. A few drops of whisky fizz dot her pink skirt. Cindy takes the napkin from under her drink and covers up the marks. Her face feels hot, and home seems far away. She finishes the last drops of liquor in her glass and clinks the ice cubes with the straw. The bald one and the other guy throw coasters at their friend, and he deflects them so they go flying behind the bar.

"What did you do, Jamie?" The bartender raises her voice and throws her arms across her Nickelback-clad chest.

"Nothing. Shut up."

Cindy reaches for her purse. She could call home and listen to the answering machine one last time before she gets with a new man. Her phone is almost dead.

"Are you okay?" The bartender grabs Cindy's newly empty glass and dumps the ice cubes.

"She's fine. I already said sorry." Jamie is teetering around like the top of the beeramid. He puts his arm around Cindy. Silent and still, Cindy tries to assess the meaning of the gesture.

"Doesn't she look fine? She looks fine." Every time he says "fine," Jamie's fingers press down on her shoulder. She thinks she likes this heavy hand. Cindy looks at the bartender, who looks back at Cindy as if she isn't fine. Maybe she should have given her a better tip.

"God, Jamie. Leave her alone. And no more fucking beeramids!"

"I was just going to buy her a drink. And maybe I don't want to leave her alone." Jamie puts the empty bottle on the bar and indicates that he wants another.

"Whatever." She stalks away to serve an old man in a ball cap.

Another coaster comes flying and hits Jamie in the back. His arm is still firmly around Cindy's shoulders.

"Mike doesn't want me talking to his woman," Jamie whispers into Cindy's ear. His breath is tart and warm. Not unpleasant for someone who's consumed enough beer to construct a beeramid and splash alcohol onto her. "She was my high school girlfriend. And she all loved me and shit. I was only in it 'cause her dad sold pot. Don't let Mike know. It's fun to piss him off."

"Oh." Cindy hopes they are all out of coasters.

Mike's woman brings over their drinks. Jamie raises his beer up for Cindy to admire.

"These are on special." Jamie's beer is still raised.

"Well, that is special." Cindy raises her whisky fizz, and Jamie knocks his bottle into it. A splash jumps out over the side and onto her lap.

"Shit. Sorry again," Jamie removes his arm, and Cindy feels empty. He wipes at her skirt with a painter's rag from his pocket.

"Why don't you go sit back down with your friends?" She could leave now. Two-and-a-half drinks seems like a perfectly respectable night. And a man has touched her shoulder with force. Jamie's arm is gone and probably also her chance to show him the sexual power of a woman with age as an asset. Even though she's a woman who hasn't exerted any sexual power in years, who actually could use a step-by-step instruction manual to jog her memory.

Jamie ignores her and sits on the stool beside her. "You look really familiar. Where have I seen you?"

"Nowhere."

She wasn't a friend's mother who had baked him cookies or the nurse who'd taken his blood. She didn't participate in community theatre or volunteer to raise money selling raffle tickets.

Jamie puts his fingers under her chin and with his painty hands, delicately turns her head toward him. He brushes the curling ironed curls, which are falling out anyway, from her face with his enormous thumbs and pulls all of her hair up and holds it in a loose bun on top of her head. A stray curl falls and lands in front of her eye. Despite his inebriation he sweeps it gracefully into his hand. His eyes look into hers. He touches her lip with the tip of his finger.

"On the roadside. Fuck, I knew I'd seen you somewhere. The side of the road near where they were blasting." He keeps his fist full of hair firmly rooted to her head, his other hand pointing at her while he speaks.

"You never look pissed off like those other road safety people, or whatever you're called. And we drive by, like, four times a day."

Cindy doesn't know what to say to Jamie. In this moment of contact she is unprepared. She hasn't even known how to leave a message on her own answering machine, what to say. Her job is a particular kind of communication. Silent. Hold up a sign, wave people along, hold up a hand, smile and nod. A call and response without her having to raise her voice. She has to be quiet and use her hands to guide drivers who so often are blasting music. No one wants to listen to what she has to say. But she has to tell them what to do. Cindy doesn't even mouth the words any more, just rolls her wrists, like a bigger, more meaningful royal wave.

"I usually drive that old paint truck. But I own a GMC. Very roomy. Got it lifted. I take it out when I'm on my own time." Jamie lets go of her hair, and Cindy hopes that her curls will bounce around her face in a pleasing manner. She tries to look at herself in the beer mirrors, but can't tell. Then Jamie leans in and he seems happy, so it must look attractive.

Cindy thinks he might be trying to impress her. Talking about his shiny truck and the spacious cab. She has driven herself tonight. He pulls back from her, taking her hand to pull her off the stool, but he stumbles and their fingers disconnect. Another coaster hits Jamie in the eye. Mike's woman comes out from behind the bar and kicks the bottles on the floor. She slaps Mike's arm and shoves him into the table. Jamie tumbles back into Cindy's arms.

"We're getting kicked out." He grabs his beer and chugs it.

"Okay," Cindy says and drops her head to her chest.

"C'mon. Let's get out of here before those assholes have to pay their tab. Drink and dash on them." Jamie pushes her off the stool, throws a hand around her waist, and ushers her out the door.

Outside the air is the same as in Brat's Pub. Warm and sticky and a little bit stale. The sun is going down over the mountains pink and lovely, like the way she feels in her skirt. This moment is a bit more romantic than when she'd watch the sunset at the end of her shift, and hope to share it with someone, and be dressed in something more flattering than a reflective vest. Jamie tips himself onto her. He needs her to keep himself upright. The number of bottles left on the barroom floor indicates that there are likely a lot of drinks making their way through his bloodstream. The weight of him fills her up again, and she puts her own arm around his waist to keep balance. His face is buried deep in her neck. Cindy thinks he must be sniffing her shampoo and perfume, which mix quite well, and not the remnants of the strong sunscreen she wears at work, which shouldn't mix with anything.

Cindy gets to her car and stops. There is still the possibility that Jamie just wants to go home and be alone. That he has a girlfriend who waits for him with the barbecue on and steaks marinating in the fridge beside the cold beer he shouldn't drink more of, but she'll let him do it anyway out of love. Maybe he is short of money and hopes that if Mike and the other guy were to catch up to them and demand money he wouldn't get into a fight if he's with a woman like Cindy.

"Why are we stopped here?" Jamie pulls her closer, even though Cindy thought they were already as close as could be.

"This is my car."

"You mean this one?" Jamie pushes Cindy up against the door and falls on top of her. He grinds into her leg. An old couple walks their dog along the sidewalk, and Cindy smiles and waves at them politely. Their dog barks, and they huff at her public display and walk off.

"Pretty nice ride. What's your name?"

"Cindy."

"Cindy, you have a pretty nice ride." Jamie's hand is on the curve of her buttocks. Cindy hopes the Spanx are doing their job. His hand inches under her skirt. Spanx are far too complicated to peel off in the middle of the street. They require a woman to brace herself.

"Thank you, Jamie. Would you like a ride home?" Cindy peels herself off and unlocks the passenger door. Jamie falls into the seat and tries to play with the radio.

"There's no music, Cindy."

Cindy thinks about buckling him up so he doesn't rattle around. She closes his door and moves to the driver's side. Before she gets in, she calls Heather.

"Hey, lady. How's your pick-up night going?"

"Good. I've got a drunk young man sitting in the passenger seat of my car. And I've had two-and-a-half drinks. I shouldn't even be driving. And I don't know what to do about anything. He rubbed his hard-on right into my thigh. He is cute and has long hair! I might just drop him off and go home and finish that bottle of Merlot. Also, how is your dad? Was his surgery successful? Are you okay?"

"Cindy. You listen to me. You got this. You take him home, you walk him to the door, and then you just put your body right up to his. If he doesn't want anything, you'll know, but I bet he does since he already had his hard dick up against your leg."

"But what if I'm terrible? Like, the whole thing is sealed shut with mortar?"

"*Cindy!!!* Does this car have music?" Jamie is yelling and pawing at the driver's side window.

"Heather, I've gotta go."

"You don't have to try hard. He's going to like it. And the surgery was fine, and I'm fine, and you're damn fine. And I love you, and text me in the morning, dammit."

Before she has a chance to respond, Heather's hung up. She opens the door and plunks herself down on top of Jamie's hand. He giggles and worms back into his seat. When she starts the car, talk radio buzzes in the background.

"Can I change the station?"

"Sure."

Jamie traces circles on Cindy's thigh while he gives her directions to his little house. She notices that the lights are off when they pull into the driveway. Jamie walks up to and then in the front door, and without prompting, Cindy follows him. He sits on the floor and removes his shoes. Cindy closes and locks the door. Jamie looks up at her standing in his hallway and doesn't tell her to leave. He grabs her calf to help himself up again, and it's just like back at the pub. Familiar and close.

"Nice house."

"Yeah. I know."

Cindy steps out of her white shoes and onto the gritty welcome mat. She holds out her hand and makes what she thinks is a seductive face but is more of a regular smile. Jamie grabs her hand, and they fall together again, the way it's meant to be. Cindy kisses the underside of his chin. It tastes like primer. She licks it a little to see if she can find a spot that's not too painty. Jamie is hard against her thigh. He walks her into the living room and throws her down on the couch. Jamie climbs on top of her, still in his paint clothes. He untucks her shirt from her skirt and then kisses her. Cindy reaches up and pulls out the elastic holding his hair in a ponytail. His hair smells like freshly cut apples. Maybe they use the same shampoo.

Jamie is having trouble with his zipper. He sits up, and Cindy bolts up beside him. He yanks at it, but it won't budge. She gets off the couch, stands him up, and easily unzips him.

This younger man is like a starter younger man. Shaggy hair and not a lot of style, what she had recently learned about style anyway. He is not Ashton Kutcher. He is not an actor with agents and managers telling him to dress better, to behave more adult while still remaining cute. Under his coveralls he wears the uniform of a regular young man: boxer briefs and a faded T-shirt that remind her of something she's lost.

Cindy can't close her eyes while they kiss. She's distracted by the mismatched couches, DVDs, flyers on the coffee table, giant speakers, empty bottles, posters that don't make sense to her. Ryan didn't have things like this when she was with him. He had an entertainment system and a leather couch and love-seat. Cindy feels lighter here though, like she's in a new world, and everything is strange and exciting.

Jamie reaches under her shirt and rests his hand somewhere near her bra clasp. If they weren't clutched together, Cindy would wave him on through with a flick of her wrist, but she doesn't know how to get him to take direction. She has to wait in the now. He yanks on it and pulls the elastic tight. She is tired. Tired of waiting. Tired of feeling like she can't have control. He can't undo a bra, unzip his own pants.

She pushes him back onto the couch, reaches behind herself, and unclasps the bra, unrolls the Spanx. Jamie stands, drops his boxer briefs, and totters into her with his hard-on swaying until she grabs and directs it. She feels rattled with his penis inside her, and then she feels like she thinks she's supposed to. Wet and excited. But worried about how fast he's thrusting, and if he's noticed the flaws in her body she tries not to examine in the fog of the bathroom mirror. Her breasts rub against his chest hair, and he jackrabbits into her pelvis.

Cindy feels him falling and straightens herself to keep him balanced. She flips back, and her hip bashes into the flimsy leg of a table. The weight of his body against her, she fights hard not to lean against this thing that won't hold the two of them up. She brushes his long hair out of her face and looks down to see that he, too, has a particleboard table with a bowl full of keys.

Jamie collapses on her, and the particleboard snaps. Keys and coins jingle to the floor. Cindy falls hard, wishing she still had a layer of Spanx to cushion her. Jamie whimpers and puts his hand to his forehead. He must have bashed it on the wall.

"Fuck. Shit. Fuck," he says.

Cindy pushes the broken table bits away from the now shaking Jamie.

"I'm sorry," he says.

Cindy reaches out to touch his back.

"Just give me a minute," he says, pressing his head into her chest.

He's just another man, Cindy thinks, as she cradles his drunken head in her arms. "It's okay. Maybe another time," Cindy says.

"Just give me a minute."

Maybe another time.

Cindy hopes that Jamie won't be sick. He's had a lot to drink. If he does need to throw up, she will lead him to the bathroom and hold back his hair, like an experienced woman. Then she will put him to bed on his side. And she'll wish that she could have finished something she started. But at least she is a woman living in the now. She started something.

But he doesn't throw up. He stands up, staggers to the kitchen, and opens the fridge. She hears the crack of a beer opening. She's still in a sweaty heap, braless and Spanxless. Through the sound of his chugging, she makes for the door, grabs her shoes in one hand, her bra in the other, and kicks the Spanx into the middle of the living room, smack dab in the middle of his mess. She won't need them when she gets home, opens the door, drops her keys on her own little table, unplugs the answering machine, and tosses it from her bedroom window.

A Beautiful Feeling

"Happy birthday!"

Joanna hands Pamela a card. Pamela delicately takes the card between two fingers and says nothing. She's holding a ribbon-wrapped succulent in a decorative pot. The card still between two fingers, Pamela holds the beautiful potted succulent out to Joanna.

"I made this pot just for you! In pottery class."

Joanna stares at the plant. A single subtle swirl of orange sorbet blooms from between rubbery leaves. It's not any occasion.

"Because you've got a dental appointment next week. Min mentioned it."

Min and Joanna are total work BFFs, rarely not together. Last time Joanna went to the dentist, her novocaine had lasted for six hours, and Joanna hadn't been able to eat anything for an entire day. Pamela took note of this.

"It's just a cleaning."

"Yes. But still. It's always better to have a gift from someone before any kind of trauma. Especially dental. When you get to your desk, you'll have this bright plant to greet you."

"Well, happy birthday, Pamela. And thank you so much for this. You're always so thoughtful."

"Oh, thank you for the card." Pamela tucks the card under her arm and walks across the office.

Pamela's sedan trunk brims with pastel-wrapped boxes. The weekend spent perusing the craft fair had inspired her. Tables full of gorgeous glass beads dangling from delicate chains, illustrated and hand-stamped cards for every occasion, small kits with special tools for drawing personalized designs on balloons. It's a never-ending supply of great giving ideas, small tokens of gratitude, ways of ensuring the people in your life know that you are there and that you care.

"Give and you always get a beautiful feeling" is a cross-stitch that hangs above the door of her craft room. She also made prints of it to hang in the common lounge at the office. And postcards in case anyone has need to send one to someone else in need of knowing they are important.

Joanna's pot wasn't exactly as she'd envisioned it. It didn't capture Joanna's quiet strength or strong work ethic in a way that felt authentic. But Pamela ran out of time. With so many other gifts to create, prepare, wrap, and distribute, sometimes a thing falls a little off the mark. It wasn't perfect, but neither is any of us. The plant itself was perfect, though. The exact plant for the angle of Joanna's desk and the temperature in the office. The plant will thrive. It will bloom on Joanna's desk for years.

Their office used to be such a dreary place. And, of course, it's still a place of business, but with a few small touches, some effort over time, it's transformed so much in the twenty years she's worked there. And why shouldn't a workspace be lovely? According to the Time Use Institute, most people spend, on average, fifty-six percent of their waking hours at work, and then for thirty-three percent of the day they're asleep. It's just reasonable and good for the soul to care for your workplace people.

Pamela starts to unload her trunk, makes a mental note to box up the slow cooker she bought last week. With no children and no husband, and no desire for either, the size of this crockpot seems a bit ridiculous, even if it was on clearance. It will serve a much better purpose at work, filling the bellies of her co-workers with healthy, homemade meals. The gift of nourishment.

Min gets to the office early to set up for Asha's baby shower. A lunch break baby shower isn't very exciting, but at least it can look like a party even though no one's allowed to slip Asha third-trimester martinis.

Laden with crepe paper and a shiny silver "it's a girl!" balloon, she unlocks the main door and goes to punch in the security passcode, but it's already been deactivated. She left last night after everyone else, because it was a slow workday with a hangover. Fuck her if she forgot to set it, and now some dirtbag is inside fucking around with their very important, but mostly uninteresting, documents.

There's a rattling noise, like someone trying to open a locked door. Then a crash like metal instruments clattering to the floor.

Min attaches the balloon to an office chair. Sets her backpack on the seat.

"Hey, fucker?! Who's in here?"

No response. She can only hear more rustling, the sound of items being stacked or packed. She flicks on the lights. Then hears a bang.

"Helloooooo!? I have been in two bar fights and one scrape on a volleyball trip."

Again, no response, but now the rush of the air conditioner has kicked in, masking noises from elsewhere in the building.

Min pushes the office chair outfitted with the balloon in front of her as a shield. At the corner, she grabs the fire extinguisher and peeks around. No one. Another bang. She screams, shoves the balloon chair down the middle of the aisle, and stomps down the hallway.

"Get out of this office!" Min shouts, barrels through the cubicles with the fire extinguisher poised over her head. She can hear someone in the supply closet. In the corner, there are canvas bags loaded up with something she can't quite see. A large and dark object blocks the door to the break room. Slowly, Min makes her way to the door of the supply closet, and from the side swings the extinguisher into the frame. Pam comes out from the supply closet, removes her earbuds and eyes the fire extinguisher in Min's hands.

"What are you doing with that fire extinguisher? I could have waltzed right into it."

Min pants and drops to the floor with the fire extinguisher. Over in the corner, she can see that the canvas bags are filled with party supplies, that the dark shape in the break room door is a mass of black-and-white paper flowers in the shape of an arch. They make her single balloon look pathetic.

"How could you not hear me yelling at you at the top of my lungs?"

"I was listening to a crafting podcast, like I do every morning."

Pamela offers to help Min get upright, but Min ignores her outstretched hand, rolls around on the carpet muttering swears. The break room looks fancy. Cloth tablecloths and jars of black-and-white jellybeans, black-and-white patterned scarves, and a checkerboard rug brought in especially for the day.

"Shit, Pamela, this is decked out. But fuck. I've been binging on horror movies."

"Oh, Min. You'll be all right. Let me make you some tea. Do you want a cookie?"

Her first boss had been stern, made everyone nervous because he valued traditional office culture, yelling when things didn't seem to go his way. There was hardly any socializing. On the walls hung cheaply framed inspirational signs left over from the eighties. Men in business suits decorated with pink and aqua neon zigzags proclaiming power, an odd angle of skyscrapers pushing success, a close-up of the front of a black Bentley to show the results of hard work.

Pamela tried to understand his way, because she wanted to do a good job. She'd gotten good grades, had secured this good job, and wanted to continue the theme of good. But after her first mistake, deleting an appendix while proofing her first-ever report, he'd exploded at her in front of everyone at the meeting.

Whenever her father had been angry, her mother would bake him something: a blueberry pie, almond cookies, a batch of muffins. So Pamela had spent her weekend baking. Her boss didn't seem to notice, but her co-workers did. Dozens of iced cookies consumed by mid-morning. They happily chomped as she happily watched their chomping. In that moment, to her the entire office had evolved into a better place.

The skateboard comes in its own case. Neon-coloured, with a custom-painted deck. The image is Min's childhood dog, Pork, done in vibrant geometric shapes by her favourite local artist. Min opens the case, looks in, closes it. Opens it and looks in again. Then she shuts the case, fastens the clasp, and places the whole thing on the lunchroom counter.

"I got a gift last week," Min says.

"Well, Min, you deserve one every week," Pamela says.

"Do I?"

Min can't take her eyes off the sturdy case. The polished

wood handle, the coppery hinges.

"Yes, of course. And, honestly, this is an 'I'm sorry' gift. I want to apologize for scaring you the other day. Usually no one comes in early. And no one helps with party set-up at that hour."

The gift is the exact skateboard style that Min had posted about on Facebook two months ago, along with the idea of paying tribute to her dog with a portrait. An expensive thing that she couldn't justify buying for herself, but hoped the hints would take hold of her girlfriend.

"I saw Elle had posted about it online. That you wanted it. And it was a post hidden from you, and she wondered if anyone had seen it in town. Well, I just happened to notice this exact thing when I was browsing on the weekend."

"It's a custom board."

"I mean, I noticed where I could order one."

Min walks over to the coffee pot and pours herself a cup, the last little bit of caffeine left in there. She rummages through the top cupboard where they usually keep Baileys stocked at Christmastime, hidden behind a giant can of coffee whitener. Someone else had gotten to it first. She shakes her head, then shakes her booze-free coffee cup, and hot splashes jump onto the counter and the floor. She tosses the last few drops into the sink.

"Are you two Facebook friends? Are you friends with my girlfriend?"

"Oh, no, no, no, no, no. But she has a public profile, so I

just went on and took a look to see what might be a good idea to get for you. It comes with a case!"

"I know it does, Pam. I'm touching it right now. I can't believe it comes with a friggin' case."

Pamela is already preparing a new pot of coffee, knows they are used to her doing it. Without coffee, their days would be less enjoyable, and she enjoys making days more enjoyable, not less.

Min grabs the handle and swings the case a little aggressively. "This is nicer than what my mom got me for Christmas. Shit!"

Pamela forgot to wash her tea mug in the morning, and before she leaves for the weekend she has to make sure it's clean, just in case it attracts mice or insects or produces a strange smell. That would not be a very nice gift for someone to find on a Monday morning. A rodent as an officemate.

"She is fucking out of control. She bought me a fucking expensive skateboard!" Min shouts.

"Min, she is not out of control. She was trying to be nice," Joanna says.

Pamela hears her co-workers talking, stops and collects herself outside the lunchroom window, sets her mouth into a smile. She sees Min throw the bottom half of a muffin against the lunchroom wall.

Pamela walks in to wash her mug, hopefully safe from flying crumbs. The water trickles over her hands, but she adds too much soap. The mug overflows with froth, and it bubbles up her wrists.

"Hello, girls. I hope you're both having a wonderful afternoon."

"Hi. How's your day?" Joanna says. Min doesn't say anything.

Pamela rinses the mug, sets it in the drying rack next to scratched Tupperware containers and barely rinsed communal plates. She pumps out a long strand of paper towel and wipes her hands on the scratchy surface.

Pamela reaches into the zippered pocket of her purse and holds out a fresh pack of gum to each of them. Their hands don't move from their afternoon coffee mugs.

"Does anyone want some? I bought a huge package, and I can only chew so much gum." Pamela whips her hands around, waves the gum in front of their coffee-clutching fingers.

"Sure. Thanks! This is actually my favourite flavour." Joanna reaches out for the gum, and Pamela hands it to her, then flicks her eyes onto Min. Pamela smiles at her, waits for a response, but Min keeps her eyes on the contents of her cup, as if she's searching in there for something she lost.

To commemorate the company's twenty-third anniversary, Pamela fills every office, cubicle, and common area with balloons. The company colours are teal and yellow and are represented evenly in each space. She had to come in at three a.m. to ensure no one would be there before her. And also to make sure she didn't scare anyone else. Min's reaction to the skateboard was not ideal. It was a bit rude. Pamela doesn't understand how someone could treat another person with indignity after they'd received something so special. Min hasn't even said a word to her since the gum incident, not even a thank you email.

In every twenty-third balloon, Pamela has left a special message and a Starbucks gift card for twenty-three dollars.

"You're a special cog in the wheel!"

"Never give up on giving!"

"A gift is from the heart!"

The new intern ruins everything. Kristen has a latex allergy, and as soon as she walked into the office everything went wrong. Joanna, as the head of the health and safety committee, calls for an ambulance.

"She can't breathe! Her skin. There are red welts everywhere," Joanna says into her cell phone.

Pamela rushes to collect some of the balloons from the intern's area, get them out of her space, and also so she can re-gift them.

"Get out of the way!" Joanna screams into Pamela's face. She stomps on several balloons in her kitten heels, and Pamela pops a few more as she stumbles to make room for her office-mates who are scrambling to help.

The girl's mouth is locked in a neutral position. Never did Pamela conceive that something like this could happen, that someone could react like this to something as whimsical and lovely as balloons.

"Oh dear," Pamela says, as she stands in the corner and watches as more balloons are popped and discarded as the paramedics rush in with the stretcher. Min kicks more balloons down the hall as they pick Kristen up from the carpet.

"Everyone, go back to your desks," their boss says. "We will make sure Kristen is taken care of, and we'll let you know how she's doing as soon as we know."

"I'll call her parents," Min says, and Joanna nods.

They both walk right past Pamela. She rushes back to her desk and tries to find out more about Kristen. How could she know so little about someone in the face of a tragedy that clearly needs to be dealt with?

She searches through emails, tries to find Kristen on Twitter, on Instagram, a website. A Google search turns up nothing conclusive. Why does her name have to be Kristen Smith? Is she even a proper millennial, with no social media presence? Who is this girl?

Pamela sits at her desk rearranging her file folders until everyone else has gone home. She creeps into the shared cubicle space, settles onto Kristen's desk chair, and begins a thorough rifling of every single nook and cranny, drawer and folder. Her desk is free of photos. Only folders full of work in her filing cabinet. The only indication that Kristen likes anything outside of work is the small pink eraser shaped like a bunny that hops over the end of an HB pencil.

Another weekend filled with essential trips to more

out-of-the-way locales. Pamela is on a quest, and it means no stopping until the goal has been reached. *Would Indiana have stopped his search for the Ark of the Covenant?* she often thinks to herself after several hours of luckless rummaging.

This time she's successful. Pamela lines the craft table with vintage fabric buttons. Each she carefully selected and has now colour-coded.

Pamela keeps an old ledger on the bookshelf underneath her hot glue guns and an arsenal of glue sticks. She re-covered the dull navy blue plastic with a child's wallpaper from a home decor shop that was closing. Small bears in business suits frozen against delicate yellow stripes. There's something cute and professional about it. Inside she tracks her spending. Each year a co-worker gets a larger gift budget. Frequenting remote second-hand shops and odd little stores is how she saves money. Then when she really needs to splurge on more elaborate special gifts she has that money set aside. Just like she did for Min. Even though it wasn't enough. She'll have to do something more. Something personal.

She fires up the glue gun and clears the table of everything that isn't going to make this her best gift yet.

"Name please?"

As the woman at the patient information desk scrolls on her computer for an interminable amount of time, Pamela adjusts her bags. Her purse keeps slipping off her shoulder as she tries to delicately balance the tote on the opposite side. It currently houses timothy grass and a small white rabbit.

A bunny is easy to come by just after Easter. So many reject-ed gifts. Such a tragedy to see a loved one's hard work thought-lessly rejected by their family. Craigslist turned up a dozen right away. This one seemed best. Unnamed yet, poor soul, and a dwarf. He looks just like the rabbit eraser on Kristen's pencil. The only downside is that she isn't able to bring the house hutch she'd worked so hard on. Too large to present to someone in a hospital. But a snuggle with a new friend is enough. That is healing.

"I don't see your name here, ma'am."

"Excuse me?"

"No. This patient had very specific instructions. Family only."

Tiny claws hook into the canvas, paw at her ribcage. She lowers the bag slowly, pulls it into her arms.

"Well, that's absurd. I am one of her co-workers."

"Are you family?"

"A workplace is like a family."

The bunny rustles around, presses her feet into Pamela's stomach, ready to bound. She rolls the top edge of the bag over itself, holds it closer to her chest.

"I'm sorry. Family. Only. You can leave her a card or some-thing here, and we'll get it to her."

Pamela shakes her head. She turns away and drops her hand into the bag, pets the soft head and ears. Gets into a smooth rhythm of stroking the fur as she walks a long way toward a door that says NO ENTRY. When she turns back around, everyone is working or staring at their phones. She pushes through the door and slips in. The next room is really a hallway, full of people in beds. She ignores them, the nurses rushing around, looks for another door. The next one requires a key card, but beside it is an elevator. She pushes the button and waits. Small powerful legs start to pummel her chest. The elevator is empty, and Pamela remembers the floor her cousin was on last year while recovering from falling out of a tree. It's all she has to go on.

On the fifth floor, she looks around to find another locked door and a nurse.

"How did you get in here?"

"Oh, I must have taken a wrong turn. I was told to take an elevator to this floor to visit a friend."

"You can't be in here."

The nurse swipes her card and points at the hallway. Pamela trips on the edge of the door and squeezes the canvas bag. A loud grunt escapes the bag, accompanied by even more intense attacks from little rabbit feet.

"Shhhhhhhhh."

"What is in that bag?"

The rabbit continues to make noises, her kicks violent, desperate. Pamela goes down the list of everything she briefly read about rabbit care. She bought the right hay, fed her pieces of apple and carrot, didn't touch her adorable feet. The sounds coming out of her are louder, more aggressive. She didn't read about this. Assumed bunnies are docile and silent: the ideal pet to smuggle into a hospital.

"Is there a live animal in that bag?"

"Excuse me?"

Pamela tucks the bag under her arm. A shrill screech responds from her armpit, and the rabbit's teeth pierce the fabric, make contact with Pamela's skin through her blouse. She screams in unison with the stowaway bunny, grabs her bitten arm, and drops everything. Now there's no screaming or grunting. The bag is still. Fragrant hay has spilled out onto the floor around her.

"I'm calling security."

"Please! I am just here to see if someone is all right! I'm very concerned for her."

The nurse is already talking to someone on a wall phone while glaring at Pamela. The words "unstable," "confused," "prohibited area" are what she can make out. She can't adjust her eyes, stares at the silent, motionless bag. Deep in her stomach a queasiness, in her chest she feels the warmth and motion of the small animal against her heart. She should have looked up more about rabbits, their fragility, their distinct communication methods. She should have been less impulsive, spent the weekend with the bunny first, taken detailed notes on her behaviour, kept a photo journal.

Down the hall, a security guard walks toward her. He looks calm and kind, not angry or annoyed. Probably the type of man who is very grateful for every gift he receives, who doesn't take generous people for granted. When he tells her that she has to leave, he reaches down to get her purse, hands it to her. This gesture secures her feelings about this man. She takes note of his name tag.

"Okay. I'm going to escort you out now."

"I just want people to feel special. I am not one to leave a mess."

He starts walking her away from the nurse, the bag on the floor. She runs from him and grabs for the bag. She swoops it up easily, because it's empty. No nameless bunny corpse. She's alive somewhere in the hospital, already abandoned twice.

"What we experienced last week was the very definition of thoughtlessness." Lisa has gathered them in the conference room to discuss the balloon incident.

Pamela can hear people whispering Kristen's name, can't quite make out what they are saying about her, if she's in the hospital, out of the hospital. Pamela had taken a few days off after her trip to the hospital. She rarely took vacations, often stayed late or arrived early, and had more days owed to her than anyone else on staff. It's her first day back since, and she hasn't checked her emails, heard any word about how Kristen is doing. Her now useless gift for Kristen, nailed and glue-gunned to perfection, is still sitting on Pamela's craft table at home.

"The health and safety committee will be creating a new handbook. There are many small violations and safety concerns that they will be taking seriously as they implement changes and create a better work environment. As well, they are looking for new members. The original team was only two members, and one of them was Kristen. Min has recently joined and has taken on the task of recruiting." Lisa points at Min, who flashes a goofy smile and waves her hand like a beauty queen.

Min and Joanna sit in front of the flower wall on the opposite side of the room from Pamela. Since the installation, the conference room has smelled of dead flowers, and she can see how many plants need to be picked or pruned. As if they can read her thoughts, Min and Joanna start plucking flowers from the wall. Each of them grabbing the deadheads. But also they're plucking fresh blooms, grabbing at the new buds and tossing them to the floor. Min pulls a mauve pansy and crushes it in her fist. Actively destroying Pamela's gift to the entire office.

"There is a card for Kristen at the end of the table. I know Kristen was our newest team member, but please sign it with your most thoughtful sentiment. As well, there's a fund to send her a gift basket, one that adheres to her strict diet and won't cause another horrific allergic reaction. Thank you all. See you at next week's meeting."

Pamela rushes to the card, wants to make sure her words are clear: "We learn from our mistakes, the best is always ahead of us. Warmth and health, Pamela."

She steps aside and sees Min's hands, dusted with pollen. Min picks up the card, gets pollen on the pristine white back. She rolls her eyes and elbows Joanna in the side. Joanna throws her a look and hands Min the card-signing pen.

"Hi, Joanna. Min, I would like to say something." Pamela steps close to them to speak.

"Is it sorry for almost killing our co-worker? Because that would be nice to hear."

"I would like to join the safety committee."

Min laughs, drops the card to the table, and doubles over. "Um. No. What about that?"

Pamela is shaking. "Excuse me?"

"No. You are not joining any committee I'm a part of."

"Min, come on, sign the card and let's go. She didn't know," Joanna says.

"And you brought in a balloon a few weeks ago, Min. It could have happened to any of us."

"It didn't happen to you. And I took your advice from your sign in the lounge. I gave away everything you've given me to the Salvation Army. Giving is great!"

"Well, I—"

"Pamela! Come into my office, please." Lisa motions for Pamela to follow her.

As she walks down the hallway, behind her she can still hear Min and Joanna talking, but can't make out a coherent syllable. Everyone muttering. She sits on a chair in front of Lisa's desk and watches her mouth move. All she can envision is the stripped blossoms, petals on the carpet being trod on.

"Did you hear me? You'll need to tone everything down, all right?

"Excuse me?"

"I think it's nice on special occasions, but right now it all needs to stop."

Her head is flooded with images: gifts still wrapped, glue guns at ease, deep frowns, her alone at home with her thoughts, dead flowers, dead dreams. No one hates a gift. Not if it's given by someone so good at giving.

After her talk with Lisa, she leaves work early. She says she has a doctor's appointment, but that's just not true. Everyone knows Pamela would schedule an appointment only before or after work, would start hours earlier to get her work done, would not leave everyone in the lurch. Her heart is beating too fast, her head unfocused. She goes straight to the craft store, pays to park her car for an entire day.

She drags a rolling cart through the aisles, examines the scrapbook papers in detail, holds paint pens up to her eye to really see the nuance in each colour. Pamela marvels at the variety of glue sticks available now, pats the perfect squares of felt, and pushes her hand into the rows of yarn, her skin immersed in textures and tones. Her heart beats less rapidly.

She turns the corner and sees a woman and her child in the ribbon aisle. It's like a painting she would hang in her living room, everything colour-coordinated to perfection. It's a favourite because of the level of organization. There are no missteps in the ribbon aisle.

"Mama, what kind of ribbon do you like best for birthdays?"

Pamela's ears perk up. She pulls her still empty basket behind her and looks at the silver ribbons.

The woman whispers to her small child that she doesn't need a gift for her birthday. "Honey, you're the only gift I need."

"Don't say that to your child," Pamela shouts. Her eyes sting with tears. The woman speaks to her, but she can't hear what she's saying, her head foggy again, her heart galloping. Tears are streaming down Pamela's face. A guttural whine escapes her body. She's staring down at the little girl, the mother's voice getting louder, and the child's small eyes also welling up with tears. She's small and scared. Pamela feels this too. A red-vested employee rushes over, is also talking, but Pamela still can't hear anything. The woman picks up her sobbing daughter and holds her face to her sweatshirt.

The staff member reaches for Pamela's arm and starts escorting her to the escalator. Pamela looks at this nice woman just doing her job, and she slaps away her arm and runs. Hand still clutching the empty basket, she winds her way through aisles, knows the way to get somewhere without anyone noticing. She's got a craft map stored in her brain. At the back of the store, she skips under the red rope and silently cries in the dark, empty craft classroom until the store closes.

The next day, Pamela goes in to check on the flower wall, make sure some of the plants are still going to survive. Something she cultivated in this office won't disappear. She can't hear the dull noise of the generator and of water being sent to their little roots.

She checks the control panel. Everything is fine. She listens again. Nothing. Above the wall, she can see slashed pipes. Someone has cut the water supply to the flower wall.

Min and Joanna walk past the conference room windows, sipping their coffees as if everything were normal. Pamela tries to make a mental note, envisions herself in her craft room. She imagines swatches and scissors and catalogues and online sales, but when she opens her eyes there is nothing bright. The wilting flowers smell like boiled compost, and her nostrils stiffen. She's unsure where to begin giving again.

"I am the most thoughtful woman here!" Pamela shouts into the empty conference room.

Hamsters

Danilo lives in the white house with the green trim. The paint is chipped, but the flakes of trim are still green, and the brown of the wood shows through. Most of the house still looks white. It was already in disrepair when his parents bought it after they arrived in Canada from Manila fifteen years ago.

Inside, Danilo's mother puts a meal together for him and his younger sisters, five-year-old Imee and Maggie, "five months until seven," as she likes to remind him. His father has to work out of town for now, somewhere up north. There were lay-offs, and he took the next job that came along. Once he makes enough money, he'll open a corner store, where Danilo imagines he will have to stack crates full of pop every afternoon.

After his mother reheats the pork and steams the rice, she will grab her purse and come outside in her scrubs to say good-bye for the night, even though it's still bright and scorching. Out front, Danilo leans on an old rake, comatose in the sun. His sisters play bad guy versus good guy, Maggie brandishing a water pistol, and Imee waving a rubbery fly swatter caked with fly guts. Danilo can't decide who is bad and who is good. Wiping sweat from his head, he thinks about which chore he can put off today and where he left his sunglasses. Rake held like a guitar, he taps out "Welcome to the Jungle" on the handle.

"I got you with my gun." Maggie is gleeful that she made a hit.

"So. That water is warm already." Imee never admits defeat.

They chase each other, run around him over and over again, as though he isn't their older brother but a tree that managed to grow out of the dead grass. The edge of the lawn is the colour of dust, but nearer the house, in the shade, the blades spring green and long. Danilo will have to mow along the perimeter of the house with the heavy electric mower.

"What's wrong with your eyes, Dani?" Maggie shouts as she passes him by.

"Nothing, Maggie. His eyes are fine." Imee starts to slow down. The shot of water has taken its toll.

"It's called squinting, twerps."

"Maggie broke your sunglasses."

"Did not."

Danilo stays still a moment, times it right, then drops the rake, swings his arms down, and scoops up the girls, one under each arm. Imee and Maggie shriek with joy.

Next door, Mr. Anducci waters his flowers and tries to ignore the shrieks. Danilo hates the garish pink and purple petals and the fact that the old man waters them every day, even though they're on water restrictions and only allowed every second day. Their mother doesn't even let them fill up their plastic dolphin pool every day. The Anduccis have had fifty years to perfect their house and yard, and the old man has a fit over any imperfection. He almost slapped Imee for picking one of his precious flowers.

"Please put us down," Maggie pleads, but he flips her over and lets her dangle upside-down at his side. Her tiny toenails glint with sparkly polish.

A newer sedan pulls up to the curb and Mr. Anducci turns off the water. Danilo puts his sisters down and checks out the car. He isn't that impressed, though he knows it has a sporty engine. When he can drive in a few years, he dreams of a less family-friendly car, something that looks cool on the outside. Mr. Anducci's granddaughter, Chelsea, opens the passenger door and leaps out into the sun, slams the door without a goodbye or thank you, and the car drives away. She swings a canvas bag over her shoulder and storms through the gate, her flimsy skirt swaying. Mr. Anducci sets his hose on the concrete steps, and she runs to his arms. When they've hugged enough, he pulls a red bill out of his pocket and presses it into hers. Danilo turns away.

"Maggie! Chelsea is here."

"Oh yeah, I see her. She's wearing a new tube top. Chelsea!"

Chelsea waves at the girls and laughs. Mr. Anducci waves at them too. No one waves at Danilo.

"Chelsea, can we play with you?"

"Please? You have the best stuff."

Even though she's thirteen, Chelsea sometimes humours Imee and Maggie. Danilo dreads dragging them home after they've been playing dolls or doing makeup at the Anducci's house. He is never invited, so he stays home and does his chores with music cranked, and sometimes he hangs out with Shane and his brothers from down the street, and they jam, or he'll stay home and practice his guitar alone. No one talks about a rock star's younger sisters.

"I'm very busy, girls," Chelsea says as she arranges the hem of her skirt.

Danilo can't stand this bitchy game girls play.

"Please," Maggie whimpers in her sweetest voice.

"We got new hamsters." Imee contributes what she thinks will be the clincher.

"Don't beg her. Let's go inside." Danilo reaches out to hold their hands, but they protest and slap him away. He dreams of new and better sunglasses and squints back up at the sky. Chelsea stands silently, checking her nails. Mr. Anducci glowers.

"Okay, tomorrow after I get home from tanning at the pool," Chelsea says. She flicks her chestnut hair, exposes bare shoulders streaked with tan lines. Danilo can't help but notice that her canvas bag digs into her shoulder, that it makes her slouch on one side. Stacks of plastic bangles weigh down her arms. They hang like uncooked strands of noodles.

"Dani! Girls!" His mom stands at their own gate, her hair smoothed into a tight bun, purse clamped in her right hand.

Imee and Maggie don't budge, eyes fixed on Chelsea, still luring them with her older girl coolness. If she was fat and wearing a T-shirt and no lip gloss, no jangly bracelets, the girls might not mention her at bedtime as if she were their own private goddess.

"Goodbye, Maggie. Goodbye, Imee. See you tomorrow," Chelsea coos and, surprisingly, waves at Danilo too before heading into the house. Mr. Anducci stays outside.

"She remembered my name."

"She remembered my name too, Maggie."

"I'm leaving, girls." Their mother tries again to get their attention.

"Your lawn is a disgrace!" Mr. Anducci is back to watering and yelling. Danilo's mother looks at the plastic toys dotting the dried-out grass.

"Sorry, Mr. Anducci. We'll clean it up. Right, Dani?"

"You don't have to apologize, Mom," Danilo says. The girls cower behind his legs.

"You *should* be sorry. So brown. It makes the neighbourhood look bad." Mr. Anducci turns his hose onto his own lawn.

Their mom pulls her keys out, and Imee and Maggie kiss and hug her goodbye. Danilo hugs her too. After she's taken off in the hatchback, he goes to confront Mr. Anducci, but despite his large belly and bad leg, he's already inside with his beautiful granddaughter and obedient wife.

At dinner, the girls gobble up leftover meat and make sculptures with their rice. They all do the dishes together, Imee standing on the counter to dry and Maggie on a stool that makes her tall enough to reach the sink to rinse. Danilo washes and puts the dishes in the cupboard. Across their battered lawn is a direct view into the Anducci's kitchen window. Chelsea and Mrs. Anducci clear plates and talk rapidly. Danilo thinks his sisters must be disappointed that her delicate fingers, more suited to giving them flashy manicures, are being used for menial labour. A plate slips from her grasp and crashes to the floor, and Chelsea picks up the broken pieces, holds them out, and apologizes. Danilo smiles and looks to his sisters, but they haven't noticed a thing, Imee too busy telling Maggie that she's rinsing dishes the wrong way.

The tape player blares Guns N' Roses. When his sisters get ready for bed they want to hear "Girls Just Want to Have Fun." Danilo cranks up "Appetite for Destruction" and pretends he doesn't know what they're talking about. They point at themselves and yell.

"Girls! Girls!"

Danilo doesn't see the value of Cyndi Lauper, but they're still young and haven't refined their taste in music yet. Rooting through the Barbie lunchbox full of cassettes, he examines each one and then tosses it back in.

"I see everyone else in here. Here it is, Madonna."

They shake their heads and yell and squeal.

"No! No! Girls! Girls!"

"Don't you like Madonna?" Danilo thinks she's a bit better looking than Cyndi, which must be why girls like girl music. To admire a pretty girl singing and want to be just like her.

"She's okay. We don't love her," Imee says, speaking for the two of them. Maggie diligently brushes her teeth in the doorway to show Danilo that she's taking bedtime seriously. After a few more fake-outs, he slides the right cassette into the player and turns the volume up. Imee jumps out of bed and rushes to get her toothbrush too. They dance in their nightgowns and sing through the Crest foam, then spit and dance and sing all over again.

He brings in their new pets, and the girls kiss the hamsters goodnight.

"Goodnight, Casey." Maggie nuzzles his brown face.

"Goodnight, Cyril Sneer," Imee whispers into his peachy fur.

"Danilo?" Maggie's voice is higher than is comfortable.

"You ask every night. You can't sleep with the hamster, Maggie."

He tucks her in tight.

"You don't know everything," Maggie pouts.

"You'll crush him."

He puts Casey and Cyril Sneer back in their home, a tall white bucket filled with cedar shavings.

"No, I won't."

"No, *I* won't because I'm so much smaller than Maggie," Imee says with a sinister giggle.

"Are you saying I'm fat?" Sensitive, Maggie pushes her whole body under the covers and whimpers. Danilo pats the ball of her covered in blanket.

"No one is fat, and no one sleeps with hamsters. And no one will get to see Casey and Cyril if you don't stop fighting and act cool."

Maggie's head pops out of her blanket. She gives him a nonchalant look and props her head up on her elbow. "Whatever you say, boss."

Wrangling the bucket in one hand, he clicks off the light and closes the door. The critters rustle in their fresh shavings. He puts their bucket in his bedroom and heads downstairs.

"I'm cool. Right, Maggie?" Imee's voice reaches him in the living room just before he switches on the TV to watch music videos.

Mr. Anducci is staring at him again. Danilo pushes the old mower over the healthy grass, careful not to run it over the cord. He's finally gotten the girls to pick up their toys and put them in the toy box, and now he's clipping the grass. Brown grass can't turn green overnight, but at least he can make all of it a similar length. Mr. Anducci leans on his hoe, looks in Danilo's direction. It makes him uncomfortable. Maybe Anducci will freak out and yell at his mom again. Maybe he's gloating about his immaculate lawn, perfect garden, and vines bursting with grapes along his metal fence. Sturdy and clean, no chipped paint, no missing posts. He should take care of their yard, share some home and garden tips instead of being a jerk.

Inside, his sisters wait for their date with Chelsea. They're fighting over who will wear the blue dress because they've decided that must be her favourite colour.

The temperature is higher than yesterday, and Danilo wishes the girls were playing outside today. Then he'd have an excuse to fill up the pool and climb in with them. If his mother wasn't so nervous about deep water, he could have taken them to the public pool where they could study Chelsea in her bikini, observe her attracting boys and brushing them off. Instead, Imee has spent all morning making a pile of clothes on the floor as Maggie clings tightly to the coveted dress. He hears their shouts through the intermittent lulls when the motor stops working and he has to kick it to start it back up. It takes pushes and kicks to use the heavy machine, the process so slow he's not sure when he'll finish. Slash and Axl don't mow the lawn. They don't have brown grass either.

Mr. Anducci hobbles out of his yard, and Danilo kicks the lawn mower for the millionth time. Happy not to have the old man stare at him while he tries to deal with this crappy chore and crappy machine, he lifts his shirt up to swipe his face. Sweat soaks through the cotton, creates a salty, black licorice smell that stings his nose, reminds him of his father. When he drops his shirt, he sees the old man limp toward the extension cord on the mower and unplug it. Danilo kicks the base hard.

"What are you doing?"

He stands tall, but the older man towers over him, even though he's shrunken over the years.

"This is not how you do it."

Mr. Anducci takes the mower from Danilo and flips it over onto its side. The blades are coated in flecks of green and may be a bit rusted. Danilo wrestles with the weight of the metal and the man to right the mower again. All he wants to do is finish the job and not have to deal with his neighbour's anger problems, and strum a few songs before reheating dinner. "Get away from my lawn mower."

Mr. Anducci ignores him, drops to the ground to fiddle with the blade. "See here, boy. This is your problem."

"What problem?"

He wavers on his bad leg, tightens something with a small screwdriver from his pocket. "Now you won't have to kick it like an angry animal."

Danilo is not the one who's angry all the time, the one getting into everybody's business. Mr. Anducci plugs the mower back in and motions for Danilo to push it. It runs smoothly, making a neat row of cut grass along the side of the house. He turns it around and pushes the other way, and there is no lull. He can't hear two little girls arguing about who's got the cuter outfit. He turns it off.

"And you cut it too short. That's why it burns."

Again, Mr. Anducci's eyes are fixed on him, even though he's already fixed the mower, gotten him to mow in the first place. The old man points to Danilo's arms. "Do you lift weights?"

A disgusted look on his face, he shakes his head.

"You are strong though."

Though he's lean, his arms are getting big. While he practices his chords, the curve of his bicep is visible, and he glances at it to check out how it looks. This summer it looks good.

"I can't move as well as I used to. I have some old pipes that I need to get rid of. I need more room for my garden. They're behind my greenhouse. You can move them out to the alley for me. Next summer I can show you how to make that better."

Mr. Anducci points his hairy hand toward Danilo's back-yard, a concrete pathway beside the carport, and a small plot of dirt dominated by a single row of vegetables, weeds, and lawn chairs. His mother only had time to properly tend the garden for the first few months of his life. Before he even ate solid food.

"I have to watch my sisters."

"It will only take a few hours. Tomorrow."

The conversation is broken by several loud thuds coming from the upstairs window, followed by crying. Danilo nods his head. He could use a break from caring for the hopeless lawn and sisters.

"I'll pay you something."

Danilo thinks of Chelsea's spindly arms, just enough muscle to hold up a fifty-dollar bill.

Dinner is Imee talking over Maggie talking over Imee. Chelsea braided their hair, and when they unravel them in the morning they will have almost-perms. That is why neither of them must get their hair wet and so can't take baths, to make sure they look their best. Nail polish remover stung her scraped thumb, but Imee pretended that it didn't because she squirmed while Chelsea drew the gold star, and it was her fault they had to start all over. Maggie made up a dance routine and sang, but not too loud, and Chelsea told her that she had a beautiful voice. Chelsea is going to give them some of her old clothes to wear.

Chelsea doesn't have a favourite colour, but she does like blue, but also red and purple and definitely pink. During the school year, Chelsea goes to catechism on the same day as they do, but across the bridge. Chelsea shaves her legs. While they talk about Chelsea, they make heart shapes with their rice.

Before bed, Casey and Cyril Sneer make a brief appearance to be kissed and brushed. Danilo puts on "Material Girl" while his sisters sing into their toothbrushes. Chelsea likes Madonna more than Cyndi Lauper.

Danilo is surprised that the Anduccis have garbage too, but not surprised that it's hidden from view. The pipes smell strange, like there's been a long-dead animal or vegetable rotting inside them while they've been stacked against the fence and pinned to the greenhouse. He's careful not to crack the plastic greenhouse wall as he hauls them out into the alley, one by one. On his hands he wears a large old pair of Mr. Anducci's work gloves. They make his wrists look like copper wire.

Cars line the gravel lane of the alley, most of them second vehicles bought second-hand for teenagers to cruise in, to and from each other's houses. Lines drip and sway with laundry in backyards. Barbecues sit idle until fathers come home to light them and throw on slabs of meat. Every evening, Danilo can smell steaks and hamburgers being grilled.

A pack of kids runs from yard to yard hurling water balloons. A stray skids to a stop behind Danilo and splats him in the back of the knee. Pipe in his hands, he turns, careful not to knock the boy out. It would have been nice if the kid had got him in the head or chest. He's boiling. Kicking out a cloud of dust, the boy jerks through a fence and out of sight. Danilo hacks dirt into his lungs. Between coughs, he hears Imee bawl, a high shriek followed by blubbering. He ignores it, drops the pipe, goes back for another. Hopefully, his mother will sleep through the noise.

"*Dani!* Help me." It sounds as though she's been in a serious car crash.

Danilo moves to avoid hitting a parked car and sees her, red-faced, in the corner of the yard. He walks over.

"Dani," Imee sobs into her closed hand.

Danilo puts down the rusted pipe and pulls Imee over the fence. His loaner gloves leave a smear of red metal dust along her pink T-shirt. She scowls at the dirt.

"Dani! Now I'm dirty too," Imee scolds him and wriggles to the ground.

"Sorry, Imee."

Danilo takes off his gloves and throws them down. One hand still in a tight fist, she examines her shirt. He knows she will make him pay for this later, for ruining her matching shirt and skirt with the printed kittens and her carefully selected matching rubber flip-flops from her basket of coloured flip-flops. It will cost him at least one dollar to ply her with a new pair from Kresge's.

"We'll clean you up."

"Fine. I look ugly now."

"You look the same."

"No."

"Why are you crying?"

Danilo watches her face change as she remembers her distress. She pulls open her tiny hand and points to her index finger. Chipped green wood protrudes from her brown skin, ringed with red.

"I got a sliver."

"Were you climbing on the fence?"

Maggie is at the fence looking on in fear. She must have encouraged whatever game caused the injury.

"We were only playing adventure models, Dani," Maggie yells from their yard.

He yanks the wood out, and Imee yelps. A stubborn piece remains under a thin layer of flesh. She looks down at it and wails.

"It ... will ... never ... come ... out," she screams between sobs.

He shushes her with a finger to her lips. She spits. "Dirty hands."

Mr. Anducci stumbles out of the house, limps out to the garden. Chelsea is right behind him, her tanned legs fully visible beneath her neatly rolled up denim shorts. She frowns at Danilo.

"What's the matter, cutie?" Chelsea trills this out, a bird's voice coming from her stiff body. She bends at the waist and puts her hand on Imee's hot black hair. The presence of the queen of girlishness calms Imee down enough to stop shaking.

"You? What did you do?" Mr. Anducci's accusations make Danilo want to run the rusted pipe through the fence.

"She got a sliver."

"It'll be okay." Chelsea pulls Imee in for a hug.

"And Dani got me dirty with his gross gloves!" Imee pushes herself further into Chelsea's body. Clinging to the fence, Maggie sings Cyndi Lauper to get everyone's attention. Each verse, her voice gets louder. Danilo thinks about what Axl Rose must be doing right now.

"If that fence wasn't such a piece of rotten shit, then this never would have happened. Are you okay, little one? Of course you're not. That place is a hazardous zone." Mr. Anducci reaches down to comfort Imee, but she jerks away from him.

Without thinking, Danilo kicks his gloves. Mr. Anducci glares at him and huffs. Imee hides from the old man and cries hard again. Somewhere Axl Rose is in a hot tub with champagne, writing epic rock and roll.

"Gianni, you need to finish eating and take your medicine. And her little hand could get infected." His wife says this from the door, fanning herself with a romance novel.

Chelsea takes Imee's uninjured hand. Maggie's singing changes to a wild rendition of "Like a Virgin." Mr. Anducci glares harder at Danilo.

"Gianni! Get in here and take your pills now," Mrs. Anducci says and slaps her romance novel against the screen door. Her husband takes a quick glance at the greenhouse before he limps back inside.

"I'll take care of you, Imee," Chelsea says.

"Thank you, Chelsea. You're so nice and so pretty."

Chelsea laughs at Imee's precociousness. Danilo watches the two girls walk to the house: Chelsea's preened hair a few shades lighter from the sun, Imee's as black and thick as ever, kinked with an almost-perm. At the door, Chelsea scoots Imee in ahead of her and waves for Maggie to come over too. Maggie climbs over the fence. One less chance for sibling rivalry.

There are still stacks of pipe piled behind the greenhouse, but Mr. Anducci gives Danilo five dollars and tells him he can finish tomorrow. He goes home and practices his finger-plucking, no girls to disturb him.

After the wound was treated, they performed one of their dance routines for Mr. Anducci, and he told them they were very talented. Mrs. Anducci packed up food for the girls to take home. They helped her make ravioli, and Imee wants to keep them in her room to show off. Danilo convinces her they should eat them for dinner instead. Maggie is proud because hers look much neater than her sister's and have more filling.

Over their handmade ravioli swimming in red sauce, the girls tell Danilo that they told Chelsea he can sort of play the guitar. Then they had an air guitar contest, and nobody won because they were all so great. The girls too hyper to be helpful, he sends them to play and does the dishes himself. There is nothing to view in the Anduccis' window but an empty dining table.

At bedtime, Imee flashes a neon Band-Aid over her sliver

wound. Maggie flashes a matching plastic bangle on her wrist. Imee whines that she left her new bracelet in Mrs. Anducci's living room. She took it off because she didn't want to get Italian food on it.

The hamsters are forgotten, and he thinks about how ridiculous it would be to bring ravioli in to be kissed goodnight. He goes down the hall to grab his guitar. His bedroom smells rotten. Hamster droppings. Cyril Sneer is sweet like always, but when he reaches his hand in to fish out Casey he gets nipped. With a quick snap he lifts him by the scruff and underneath his white belly is a mound of pink. The babies are hideous, and even though they squirm and squeak, their eyes are closed, and they look dead. Remembering the ravenous mother who ate her babies and the angry father who almost killed her in the kindergarten classroom, Danilo drops Casey back into the bucket. He makes Cyril Sneer a new, smaller home out of an ice cream pail, an ashtray for a food dish. There is no extra water bottle, so he uses an empty jar lid. Cyril will just have to make do.

Downstairs, Danilo sits in the quiet heat of the evening. This summer is almost over, but maybe next summer he could get a real job, and he won't have to work for his father counting out change for popsicles. His guitar playing will be killer by then too, and maybe he can start a band with Shane and his brothers. An all G N' R cover band until they write some of their own songs. He'll have to get an electric guitar.

He hears a knock at the door. Shane and his brothers are at the family cabin, and no one else would come by so late. He opens the door, and Chelsea breaks the night in a breezy sun-dress. A nervous grin on her face, she holds out a lime green plastic bangle to him.

"Imee forgot this. I gave it to her."

Danilo takes the bracelet from her, heavier than he imag-ined it to be. She looks over Danilo's shoulder and into his house.

"Thanks."

"Is that your guitar?" Chelsea pushes past him and heads for his guitar sitting on the couch. She sits beside it and puts her arm around it, rests her head on it and looks at it lovingly.

"It's like your date."

"Thanks for bringing this over."

He tosses the bangle onto a chair but stays by the open door. Chelsea moves away from his guitar and sits up straight. She folds her hands into her lap. He plays with the doorknob and watches Chelsea make herself comfortable on his couch, in his house. With her own bangled hand, she pats the seat beside her and smiles. Her teeth are the slightest bit crooked. He shuts the door.

"Come and play something."

"You've never even talked to me before. Ever." He picks up his guitar and sits on the other end of the couch, rests his in-strument on his knees.

"I thought you probably think that I'm immature or some-thing."

"Why?" Danilo looks at her smoothly shaven legs. They are

very similar to his own, thin with hints of muscle running down them. That sucks.

"You're just such a quiet guy. And I play with your little sisters all the time." She looks down at her folded hands.

"So?"

"I like them. They're sweet." Chelsea looks over at him, his guitar resting uselessly on his legs. "I like guitar music." Her voice is bright.

"You like pop music."

Danilo strums a few bars of "Material Girl." Chelsea laughs, and Danilo stops playing. She grabs the neck of his guitar.

"No, I like it. Keep going."

"No. I don't know it very well. I don't practice it all the time."

"What do you know well?"

"You won't like it."

"Just play it." She kicks his leg and bumps the guitar on his lap. It twangs and tips, and he grabs it before it hits the floor. Careful with each chord change, he plays a very slowed down version of "Welcome to the Jungle" and mouths the words. Chelsea sways to the music. He screws up and starts over. Then he screws up again. He finally gets through the first verse and puts down his guitar.

"I like it better that way." Chelsea lays down on the couch, her feet crossed in the air.

"I'm just learning, so I can't play it like it sounds on the record. I'm not Slash."

"That's okay." Chelsea pats him on the leg.

"The album only came out about a month ago."

He sets his guitar on the floor. She stretches her arms out in front of him, and he tickles her the way he does when his sisters get tired and yawn and stretch. Chelsea laughs and tries to grab his arms away, but he's stronger than she is. Her body twirls and twists, and when Danilo stops tickling she lands with her head on the arm of the couch, her body lying across his lap. She slaps him lightly on the cheek. She looks relaxed, and Danilo feels relaxed too.

"Can you play 'Papa Don't Preach'?"

"I don't know that one."

"It's on the newer album."

"My sisters don't have the newer album."

"I'll make them a copy."

"Please don't."

They both laugh. She won't stop making eye contact with him. He can't stop smiling at her crooked smile. He wants to reach down and touch her smooth legs, but instead leans in and kisses her. The arms he thought were so weak a few days ago wrap around his neck and hold on tightly. They stop for breath and look at each other. Danilo looks to see if Chelsea is going to hesitate, decide that he is unworthy, run away. She doesn't. He wishes he'd put on a tape, kisses Chelsea's warm lips again. She continues to grip his neck.

The sound of a running hose breaks through their kiss. Hard streams of water against the wall of the house. Dani chances to open his eyes and through the slit between the curtains sees Mr. Anducci stationed across the fence. In his own yard, he's got his hose pointed at Danilo's lawn. He drowns in another kiss, but the sound of water beating against his home distracts him. The guitar drops to the floor, and he gets up.

"What's wrong?"

"Nothing. I think I hear my sister crying."

"I don't hear anything." She moves toward him, puts her hand on the crook of his thigh. He blocks it.

"She has a soft cry."

"Which one? They both wail."

She laughs. He feels the pressure of her hand on the cotton of his shorts, but it's like she's touching underneath the fabric, underneath his skin, underneath the place where songs come from.

"I've got to go check on them."

Dani shifts, pulls up the neck of his guitar between his legs, separates the bare flesh of their summer skin.

"I can wait," she says, lounging with an arm above her head, cradling a bouquet of her hair.

"No. They take forever to get back to sleep."

"Fine."

She gets up and adjusts her strap back onto her shoulder, walks across the room stretching her arms high, exposing another few inches of thigh. Dani sinks into the couch, crushes his palm against his leg.

"Shit."

"What?"

"My nonno is outside. He can't see me in here." She plops back down beside him on the couch. "He wants me to marry a nice Italian boy."

"We're not getting married."

"Not that there really are any."

She slides her body down the couch so she's almost vertical. An errant leg kicks; her toes strum the strings, a long, messy note. Dani stops the sound with his hand.

"They're all so selfish. With their cars and their biceps. And their moms. Nothing closer than a mom to her son. Momma's boys. All of them. Trying to please her while they wait for her to serve them dinner and stuff. At the table waiting for food in their stinking clothes. It's not worth it. But that's what they all do."

With a wriggle of her toes, she strums the guitar again. "Everyone expects me to be a mom in five years. I can feel it."

Danilo's mother was seventeen when he was born, close to eighteen, but not quite. His parents got on a plane, got away from their old lives, before he needed luggage.

"Shit. I can't go out there."

"Well, I'm going up to check on them."

"Fine. Shit."

"He won't care."

The look she gives him says that he will care. A lot.

"Wait outside the back door."

"Boring," she says but picks herself up. At the door she tries to kiss him, but their heads move away at the same time. Neither one apologizes. Or says goodbye.

Through the door, he can hear her quiet breathing, the waiting. He creeps upstairs. Out the hall window, he can see Mr. Anducci's changed direction, trying to nourish the vegetable garden, the stream jumping the fence. Danilo's property drowning. Chelsea hasn't emerged from his yard yet. He assumes she'll wait in the darkness until her grandfather packs it in for the night. Instead she pulls around the far corner of the yard and comes through the back gate. Mr. Anducci turns off the hose, and brings her into his arms. She stands in his embrace, and Dani can tell that's she lying about something. They go inside. In the kitchen window, he watches Mr. Anducci gesture to Chelsea and his wife, and they hustle to the fridge. He looks away, walks down the hall to the girls' room.

He presses his ear to his sisters' door to check that they aren't awake. Still asleep, no cross-bedroom chatter, no bedspring squeaks from restlessness. They are sound asleep, worn out after a long, stimulating day. He heads to his own bedroom, sets his instrument under his bed, and throws himself on top of it.

Danilo wakes up in his clothes to squeaks from the bucket. Instead of two hamsters there are a dozen, Cyril and Casey not boys after all. He must have touched some of the babies earlier when he fed them, because Casey has eaten two of them. The others wriggle in the blood of their departed siblings. Danilo finds them so strange. They look like baby moles. They could be baby anythings. They look barely alive, but someone will have to take care of them too. In the ice cream bucket, Cyril Sneer is scratching to get up the side, sliding down, trying again. At night, they have the most energy, rustling and playing until morning. He takes Cyril's ashtray, dumps out the food, and uses it to scoop up the remaining newborns.

Through the kitchen window, Danilo sees that all of the lights are off in the Anduccis' house. He goes out the kitchen door and into the night. He doesn't know what time it is. It's finally cooled off. With a steady hand, he throws the babies one by one over the fence. They land between the neat rows of the garden. Danilo can't see them once they've landed, their thin bodies hidden by lettuce and zucchini leaves.

Sometimes Imee and Maggie don't remember they have two hamsters. They won't get to meet the newborns, with their skin pink and quivering like Chelsea's lips. He'll have to break the news to them that Casey is a she and not a he. Danilo is sure they'll be thrilled to have another girl in the house.

Haul

Persona: Test Video

Camera is small. Frame. Small. Close. Not too close. Small frame. A small girl is framed. Short. Propped up on nautical striped pillows. Her sensible decor not visible through the lens of her webcam. Her face, though. Yes. Cheeks ripe as genetically engineered peaches and of a similar colour. Orange and red and pink and purplish tones along the ridges of her round cheeks. Lips lined a little sloppily, lipstick steadier. Revlon Plum Velour, a drugstore staple. Gloss is L'Oréal Colour Riche Le Gloss, in Golden Splash. Cream shadow is Sunset, M A C. $19. Discontinued.

She smiles and pulls back, forces her cheeks and lips not to strain against her fake presentation. The face of someone who always excels at things but is trying something for the first time. A tightness in the jaw. Unpolished fingers fidget with something just out of frame. She holds up a skirt with bronze shimmer-thread woven through it, the pattern like fireworks. She wants to explode.

Haul Index

Three-button blouse. Red. Polyester. $12.99. On sale. Forever 21. Will match navy, black, stripes, polka dots, some florals. Would look good for school presentation days.

Jeans. Indigo. Stretch. $39. Not on sale. American Eagle. Can wear on weekends to visit family but not for special occasions, birthdays, holidays, etc.

Jeggings. Light wash. V. stretchy. Denim/cotton/spandex. $19. On sale. Forever 21. Casual wear good for winter months with long sweaters, or as transitional pieces for fall.

Necklace. Chunky. Gold-coloured. $6.95. Not on sale. Forever 21. Will match all colours.

Skirt. Mullet. Diamond pattern. Multicoloured. $8. On sale. Forever 21. Will match a variety of pastels and primary colours. Can wear to school or on special occasions.

Note

According to *Seventeen*, mustard and gold can be worn together. August photo spread "Fall into Colour," page 58.

Reading and Research

Vogue, August and September issues, current year. What to research: boots and coats, pattern mixing. Take notes on how to discuss different types of stripes.

Teen Vogue, May–August. Current year. What to research: denim and leather, lace and feathers. Take notes on names for varying lengths of pants and skirts.

Nylon. All issues, current year. What to research: edgy style, personal style, not following trends. Take notes on what "edgy" means.

Seventeen, September issue. What to research: Fall trends, all. Take notes on which trends will potentially play out best through video presentation.

Complete twenty #ootd studies and analysis reports per week. Watch shopping haul videos by *Candy Girl*, *Becky123*, *Sure-Star99*, and *GorgeousGirlStar*. Take notes on presentation and clothing selections. Do not pay so much attention to hair.

Update: Research of blogs revealed that most popular videos are not perfect. Use bad lighting. Well, not as good. A bit grainy too. But don't want face to look shiny or greasy.

Day Planner
September 2—Shopping trip. Oak Valley Mall, Central Plaza, 8th Avenue.
September 4—First day of high school. Do not want to try too hard. Will wear old jeans and favourite tank top. Maybe new red flats, as old black flats have a hole. Though black flats are also favourite. Will make new first impression.
September 18—Group science proposal due. French test.
September 23—Movie club. Social studies assignment due.
September 29—English essay. Update Haul Index. Review Notes.

Notes
Budget looks good. Birthday stockpile still has some left over, since Grandma's card was late, and she felt generous. Will ask

for money to go to the movies. Research plots of current teen movies. Become a haul keener. Become a style keener. Become friends with two girls.

Catalogue

Dim light. After homework, after dinner, after teeth are freshest, hair brushed down. She showers at night, keeps mornings free for homemade mochas and closet organization. She films herself doing the part she likes most. Eyes trained on a rainbow-coded spreadsheet. Cells filled with important information. The most important. Documents filled with notes. Goals typed in bold red textboxes: stay organized, make good impressions, try hard, be seen. Hands stampeding over her keyboard, keeping track of school work and this new work in equal measure. Key clacks are more interesting than piano lessons, than Taylor Swift's "Trouble." It's music, composition.

Presentation 1

Drape garments over arm. Discuss fabric, colour, design elements.

No.

Presentation 2

Reach into bag and present each garment with both hands. Twirl garments, from front to back. Hold garments in front of body.

No.

Presentation 3

Use arms for manual zoom. Bring garments close to the cam and then back again. Make sure all of the pieces are shown in full. Hold garment in front of face.

No.

Notes

Revisit presentation folder for further presentation ideas. Watch clips of previous presentations. Take further notes. Put notes in "Notes" folder.

Revisit "Don't Leaf This Alone! Cardigans the Colour of Fallen Foliage!"

Words to Use

1. Cute
2. Fun
3. Flirty
4. Stylish
5. Cool

Haul Video, September 15

"Hey, everyone. I'm new to posting, but I'm a longtime fan of so many of you, and you make some awesome videos. It inspired me. Thank you so, so, so, so, so much. First, I'd like to show some tops things I got at the Gap. This one is fuchsia with polka dots and buttons all the way up. This one is yellow and printed with tiny foxes. So cute. Also buttons all the way up. Both are cotton blends. I also bought two T-shirts, one in green, one plain black, but both cute and, like, soft. Nice. One pair of leggings in Navajo green and red and yellow. Same trip, I got these jeans with zippers on the ankles, indigo wash. Copper zippers. Oh, no. They're from Old Navy. Oh, no. Ok. The jeans are Old Navy. Can't believe I got that wrong. Thanks for watching and stay stylish!"

She uses the first presentation method mixed with the second. Reaches in with both hands. Discusses fabric and colour. Drapes garment.

She stutters a little. Voice a slight quaver, her face is stiff. Stiffer than she wants it to be. Eyebrows look like tight crochet pasted above her eyes, wide and wanting. Her arm juts into the frame and clicks off.

This one, she will broadcast the next morning. No edits. One clean cut. Keep it simple. Straightforward. Just like studying for an exam.

Notes

After watching video, there are three things. Be yourself. Be yourself. Be yourself. Also, try not to do that thing with the eyebrows. Turn the overhead light down a little more. Use bedside lamp.

No comments on video. Retweet every second day.

Haul Index

Shoes. Brogues. Patent. Pleather. Silky laces. Two-toned purple and teal. $28. Forever 21.

Boots. Dark brown. Leather. Flat with side zippers. $80. Aldo
Ballet flats. Black with zebra print stripes. Faux suede. $14. On
sale.
Heels. Purple. Faux-suede. One-inch height. Detachable gold
bow. $25. On sale. Urban Outfitters.
Toms. Grey. $60. Foot Locker.
Slippers. Fluffy. Hello Kitty-shaped. Cotton and fleece. $18. On
sale. Claire's.

Notes
Overbudget. Had to borrow money from sister. Parents will
not give more money. Will do extra chores for two weeks. Most
things bought on sale. Will try and be better about sales.

Haul Index
Satin, chiffon, boning. Cocktail dress. $120. On sale. Club Mo-
naco. So fancy. Will look great on camera. Must have. Did not
even try on.

Day Planner
October 1—Math test. Science dissection. Review monthly
Haul update.
October 10—School dance. Not going. No one asked if go-
ing. Despite recent purchase of satin, chiffon cocktail dress. See:
Haul Index. Create resumé.
October 16—Shopping trip. Apply for jobs at stores you do not
purchase clothes at. Skip social studies group project meeting.

Project due in one month.

October 24—English essay.

October 31—Too old to trick or treat. Hand out candy.

Catalogue

The sun is still down when she wakes up. By computer glow, she makes a new column in the spreadsheet. Date worn. Most of them read the same. Never worn, never worn, never worn. She checks for new followers. Four on Twitter. Her hand reaches out to tap the screen, though it's not a touchscreen. A finger brushes lightly over each of the new avatars. In her oldest hoodie, she grabs her backpack filled with worksheets: some created by her, some her teachers. Downstairs, the smell of hot cereal and her older sister's complaints about how high school has made her sister even weirder.

Haul Video

"Fall is here and this is the all-shoe haul. Feet are important. Keep yours looking and feeling great in this fantastic footwear."

She details every element of the shoes. Colour, texture. She has them fly around her head like sartorial spaceships. She is enthusiastic. She memorized this script. Verbatim. She read it verbatim.

Notes

Must remember, what happened can't happen again. Parents almost saw. The closet door needs to be able to close. Fully close.

Tight. Must remember to sell items on Craigslist. Save up for necessary leather jacket. All the other girls are showing their leathers.

Comments are positive. People like her enthusiasm. She is still not herself, but people like her.

Persona

Jittery. She tries to coax the clothes into the plastic tubs, into the segmented cloth baskets, into organization. Shirts spill from the top shelf of the closet, pant legs peep out from plastic shopping bags kept under the bed.

Unworn dresses in the closet hide behind coats that rudely bulge. She layers clothes on hangers, fits the fresh tags into necks and sleeves. Bulky bodies. They are her and not her. These clothes still smell like packing peanuts, saran wrap slips, and cardboard. But she went in and bought them.

Notes

View count is up by two hundred. This is good news.

Comments are half complimentary, half creepy.

Ten new Twitter followers. Only two are bots this time.

Day Planner

November 3—Book report. Read something short. A novella.

November 13—Social studies presentation day.

November 20—Math test. Shopping day. Pick one mall only. After school.

November 24—English assignment due. French quiz.
November 26—Window shopping. No purchase. Get smoothie for energy.

Catalogue

She did not show up for her Social Studies presentation. Spent day at the mall doing research. Watching girls in their twenties walk in and out of stores. Their confidence, their legs and arms in motion, laughs and nods. Observing the motion of skirts, listening for the rustle of wool coats and scarves.

She takes photos with her phone. Click, click, click. Scrolls through. She wants a new skirt, a new sweater, a collar necklace in silver and gold. She wants an Orange Julius.

Her parents went into her closet last night to hide Christmas gifts for her sister, and everything became clear. Plastic bags full of clothes with tags, unworn sweaters, shoes in boxes. They said her neatness, organizational skills, intelligence wasted on this nonsense. She is not getting anything for Christmas. She might still pass Social Studies.

Haul Video, November 25

"It's one month to Christmas, so I treated myself to cute and flirty sweaters. If sweaters can be flirty. This has hearts on it, so it's much flirtier than this one here."

She tosses the heart sweater onto her bed like it's nothing.

"This striped one I picked up on sale at H&M. So cute, right? Yeah. It's—"

178

A sigh. Silence.

She keeps filming, nods her head, keeps it close to her chest for too long. An awkward silence in a shiny visual medium.

She stands, head still down, walks with her back to the camera, opens the closet door. She pushes the clothes back with both hands as though opening the doors to a saloon. Inside the closet, she burrows into the fabric, the colour-coordinated shopping bags, the hung dresses, boxed shoes. Her body shifts and folds to fit. Her head slips between a cardigan and a sundress. Cotton, polyester, and wool blends crowd her. She backs in further, the vibrant material a curtain. Against the back of the closet she presses her shoulder blades into the wall, makes herself as thin as a flimsy skirt. Invisible to the lens, she can still see the green glow of the camera through the fabric until her body is fully woven into the tangle of textiles.

 Nest

Sara rounds fine sandpaper over the curve of a domed wooden roof. The sides of the structure are curved as well. The house designed to look round and soft, not sharp. A request made by her client. This is just the model, what she brings to clients for inspection. First comes the initial consultation, then a scale drawing for approval, then proper blueprints, and then the scale model for approval. If all goes well, Sara will make just under $20,000 for creating one doghouse. Since her business, Barki-tects Pet Designs, opened over a year ago, she's made a dozen pet homes and now has contracts for a dozen more in the next six months.

Today's meeting is with a client and her Pomeranian. Even though the dog is small, the paycheque is big. She often finds pet size is disproportionate to the amount of money an owner is willing to pay for a designer pet home. They consider their toy pets more in need of protection. Mrs. Doty specifically asked if there was any way of making the house in the shape of Posh's favourite toy. She gets out of the car and brings the model to the front door, rings the bell. Hopefully, it'll look enough like a hot dog in a bun to please Mrs. Doty and chipper Posh. From behind the heavy oak door, she can hear both of them scuffling to the door, the lilting pant of their breath, and the yips they use to communicate. A few sighs and oohs and aahs is all Sara needs to return home elated to celebrate another design success with her wife, Kate.

That night over dinner at the Izakaya place, she tells Kate about the contract, that they're almost stable enough. Almost enough to really pursue this baby, seriously talk to their doctor, seriously consider Kate's dream. Kate wants to be pregnant, carry Sara's egg and donor sperm inside her, feel the beat of a little Sara stir. Sara's doctor says her eggs are ready when she is. The cost has always been a concern. The cost of high-end sperm and in vitro is as expensive as several pet mansions.

"Almost? You're raking it in, babe. Raking in money."

"I have student loan debt."

"So does every asshole with a graduate degree," says Kate.

"You're right."

"I know. I'll start making the appointments."

In a city of never-ending construction, a never-ending real estate bubble, a never-ending supply of nouveau riche, Sara didn't think studying architecture would be a mistake. Her wife agreed, believed in the creative potential of Sara. When they started dating, Sara had made a tiny replica of Kate's childhood tree house, the one she'd lost in a brushfire. From a grainy photograph, she'd reproduced the tilted floor, the slope of the roof, the frayed rope that swung below the entrance, the two-by-four steps nailed to the tree. Kate was in awe of how perfect it was. It felt like she could crawl right into it and read Archie comics until sundown.

Sara dreamed of creative housing, interesting and unique. Recycled materials, stability, shape, colour. She saw images in her head that would enhance the glass and concrete landscape. She graduated and looked for a job and found there was very little out there, and what was there wasn't top shelf work. No one wanted to hear her ideas on brightening the urban image of the city. But more than anything, she needed to make money, needed to find a way to make Kate not regret all her encouragement. Feisty Kate, who'd worked and waited years to live her own dream of raising little Katelets and Saralets. She'd promised Kate that after graduation they could start a family. On graduation day, Kate high-fived her and kissed her, whispered in her ear that they were going to be the coolest moms.

Months later, she caught up with her adviser, Jed. Talking to him, they'd tried to think of answers to this problem. Over eight-dollar lagers they discussed all the same old things, the way to edge ahead in a competitive market. Where were the new ideas? Where were the new ways of making a name? Could there be a new Ando, Erickson, Gehry? Sara joked that she might as well design for dogs. Jed ordered another round to celebrate.

"Celebrate what?" Sara said, tipsy and distressed.

"Your new career. Architect to the dogs."

A little research revealed that the pet industry is an area of growth. Pet supplies, pet care, pet bakeries, pet masseuse, pet estheticians. No one had ventured into high-end, one-of-a-kind, designer pet domiciles. It was an untapped market. With financial help from Kate, they developed their business plan. They pulled it together so quickly that there was no time for Sara to question her decision. The name was a post-coital masterpiece. The two of them naked and sweaty on the living room couch in the summer heatwave, when Sara made a loud, throaty orgasmic exclamation. Kate looked up from between Sara's legs and started barking. Knew they had the branding figured out. Kate pushed her in the right directions. The website was cute but not twee, interactive but not annoying.

"We're good at working together," said Kate. "This is how we'll be as parents. Look how we collaborate on this shit? We killed it."

Sara spends the next morning organizing her day planner, checks that she has all her appointments in both her paper and digital planners. Kate has left a Post-it note on top of Sara's day planner:

> *Remember. Sperm meeting, Monday, 3:20. I took the*
> *day off. xo*

She had forgotten. Kate probably saw it wasn't marked on the calendar but a client was. She texts Kate: *I have a mtg Mon aft.*

Kate responds: *I know. But really? Important?*

Sara stares at the question marks, their judging little swoops and dots. She'll cut her meeting short. She has to.

I'll be there, she texts back, *xo*

Sara spent two years applying to schools and failing to get in, then four years of grad school, six months' worth of unemployment, another eight of unsteady income, all told more years and months of waiting than Sara thought Kate would put up with. Now that Sara is finished pursuing her dream, it's time for Kate to fulfill hers.

Sara knew they should have talked about it more. That during all the nights she spent locked away in her studio across the yard in their garage, all the mornings she crawled home to sleep while Kate assessed insurance claims, there was another person waiting at the end of the timeline. A little person that they would bring into their home and feed and take care of.

The more Sara thought about it, the more she considered this person a stranger, an interloper. They worked well together; they made things happen. Without Kate's commitment, there would be no Barkitect firm. This person might be cute, but there would be interference.

"We nailed it," Kate says, clutches Sara's calloused fingers in her manicured ones.

The appointment with the fertility clinic had been very encouraging.

"Gonna get us some spermatozoa, gonna implant that in my lady bits," Kate says.

"Don't get cocky."

"I'm not cocky, I'm confident. Your doghouses are blowing up our bank accounts, and now I'm going to be one of those glowing ladies who gets to be offended and pleased when other people want to touch my bulging belly."

"You're not pregnant yet."

"No shit, honey."

Kate dances around the car while Sara scrambles in her bag for her keys. Kate humps the front of the car and makes gestures toward her flat stomach. She's beautiful, healthy. She's funny, even in these moments when Sara wants her to stop squirming and sit quietly in the passenger seat, listen to talk radio while Sara drives. There are times while Sara renders drawings that she stops to think about how sexy Kate is, how her hip juts out while she tosses sweaters from the closet, the way her lower lip droops with concern. Her auburn hair in an explosive braid each morning makes it hard for Sara to leave the heat of their bed. In a few months, she will swell and stretch; hormones will tread all over her body, and Sara won't know who this person is. Two strangers. One inside Kate, the other someone she used to know.

"The woman seemed sketchy to me," says Sara.

"She seemed sketchy? You talk to women who dress their dogs like Scarlett O'Hara and offer you money to build canine-sized Taras and milk bone fountains. And the highly educated doctor who's going to squirt some baby juice our way is sketchy?"

"She had a weird haircut."

"She had a bob."

"It was threatening."

Sara rushes across town for her next appointment, has to park blocks away and run; her short, sideswiped bleached hair flips into her eyes as she tries to run, not run. Her undercut keeps her head from building up with sweat. The client, May, wants to meet in a small park downtown. She told Sara she'd be standing near a tree on the north side. She's asked Sara to construct a home for a bird. On the drive over, she belts out classic rock, lets the radio blare, gets pumped. She's never worked with metal before, but is excited for the chance to try, add another mode to her arsenal. It must be an ornate cage, something grand. She already has a line on some scrap metal she can upcycle into something Victorian. The woman mentioned in her email that she was interested in something classic and traditional.

A small woman with straight black hair wearing a cream coat stands next to a tree. This must be her. Sara walks over to her and holds out her hand. May points up at the tree.

"Hi, I'm Sara. Thank you so much for considering my services. I've never designed anything for a bird before. Mostly dogs and cats, some rabbits, a chinchilla once."

"Shhhhh," the woman says.

"Sorry. Would you like to sit on the bench over there and discuss ..."

"Please. Just be quiet for a moment."

Sara stays silent and waits, tries not to stare. The air is warm and smells of bark and cotton. She notices that there are two clouds in the sky, each one bulbous, like cartoon clouds. Sara looks back to May, who twists her mouth and a strange trill comes out from between her lips. A small, dowdy bird emerges from the tree and lands at May's feet. The little brown thing hops about near the woman's pristine velvet flats.

"She doesn't live in my house, but we're close. I wouldn't consider her my pet, but we have a relationship."

"Excuse me?"

"I want you to create a home for her. I want her to come live with me. It's time. Something inside that will make her feel at home. Classic. Natural. Only materials a real bird would use. No substitutes. Authentic method of construction. I've been studying bird homes."

Sara feels pricks of heat in her cheeks. Is this woman mocking her? Is this Barkitecture backlash? Even Sara's surprised it's taken this long for someone to have a go at her. As ridiculous as she knows her business is, she always assumed the few online comments about her business would be the extent of negativity she'd experience.

"Why are you wasting my time?"

"Excuse me?"

"You'll still have to pay for this consultation."

"Of course. And then another payment after you've submitted the drawings. And the model, and then the final product. I think the best way to proceed is to develop a solid schedule and payment plan, don't you?"

May moves to the base of the tree, and the bird cocks her head up. Kneeling, May reaches out a hand to stroke the bird's tiny tail feather. It doesn't look at ease, but it doesn't fly away.

This woman is serious. Sara falls into the bench, rubs her eyes to stop her head from spinning.

"I'll know if you're somehow faking it," May says.

Faking it. What does it mean to authentically create a bird's nest? Bold as she can be, as innovative as she is, Sara can't imagine what this project will be like. There are levels of questioning herself that she doesn't know if she can overcome.

"I'm not sure I can do that."

"Well, there's $100,000 in it for you."

Sara watches May watch her bird. On May's arm is a designer handbag. The bird's brown feathers match the tones in the Coach logo. They look coordinated, like women and their lapdogs. Sara wonders what a bird would look like in a Juicy Couture jacket.

"I have the money. If that's what you're worried about."

"It's not the money," Sara says, even though part of it is.

"I've seen your homes. There is something special in them. I want something special. I want to know that we are going to be happy together, that someone has taken care to make something that doesn't *feel* like home—that *is* home."

Sara isn't sure how anyone could know that this small brown bird is the same small brown bird, when all brown birds look the same. May stands, and the bird ruffles and takes off. May's eyes, dewy with love, watch her land on a branch to preen. Then a second later, the bird leaps into flight. May's whole body turns as she watches the small brown spot disappear in the sky.

"Okay," Sara says, "I want to do it."

Sara tells her about the bird, the woman, the cashmere coat, the paycheque as she scrubs Kate's back in the shower. Kate is thrilled.

"What if I fail?" Sara asks Kate, backed into the shower stream.

"Are you kidding? If anyone can make an authentic bird-house for an eccentric woman with more money than brains, you can."

Soaped and slick they reach for each other, Kate panting with excitement as they kiss, as Sara reaches between her legs, a celebration of fresh ideas and clean skin.

Every day, Sara traipses through the park, studies the bird. She's energetic, sometimes frantic, in the way she moves from grass to tree. Larger birds seem unsure about venturing. For hours, she watches the finch hop along the grass or the busted stone fountain. Sara hasn't asked May if she's anthropomorphized this bird, but it doesn't seem like her way. Sara can't help it, though.

She makes notes, sketches twigs and grass, imagines the way they'll fit together in a nest. She searches for empty nests while she and Kate walk to get groceries or gelato or new socks. And just like in grad school, she spends her nights in her studio, drawing, rendering, thinking, rethinking. She questions every move she makes. The library becomes an oasis. Structure, shelving, books, kiosks.

On the way to their doctor's appointment, Sara stops

several times on the street, catches glimpse of twigs in trees. Examines them.

"See. These are not finch nests. Too sparse. See the way this looks like it could break apart?"

"I'll break you apart if you don't move faster. Someone else will snatch up this appointment if we don't get there on time. I am getting the fullest physical and fertility assessment that money can buy."

"Sorry, I didn't know we were late-late."

"What if it starts with you getting distracted and we miss this appointment, and then we miss all the important ones, and in the end someone takes my baby-making cocktail?"

Sara stops walking. After a few steps, Kate realizes she's huffing along on her own and turns. Sara's look is supposed to say, "Are you serious?" but, more likely, Kate thinks Sara's calling her an idiot. Kate's look tells her that she is serious, that they need to hustle. That she doesn't give a shit about finches.

"I thought you might be interested in this. It's an intricate project," says Sara.

"If we're not ten minutes early, we're late."

The curves of the nest are at odd degrees. There's no symmetry. Everything is angled to confuse. And each nest so different. Each finch as finicky as a West Vancouver housewife asking her to incorporate bunk beds for Persian kittens.

Immediately Sara has gone into research mode. Unsurprisingly, the females, of which May's bird friend is one, are doing the hard work of building the nest. Nice bird women in their unflattering brown house-feathers forming a comfortable cup-shaped home for their families to enjoy. To keep it all together, sticks and grass, twigs and leaves. For comfort, feathers, and, like in any good home, a bit of collected debris. There are thousands of pages of information on finches, their ways, the people who love to watch and court them with seeds and berries. Mostly vegetarians. No way to woo a finch with a pulled pork sandwich.

May approved the drawings, sent the first $25,000 the day after Sara hung them from the park bench and walked May through the construction procedure.

"I feel good about this," she'd said to Sara.

"Thank you," was her response, but what she wanted to do was an impression of Kate, running down the length of the park, arms thrown in the air, a joyful flailing of limbs.

The last appointment hadn't been ideal. They have to go back to find out the results. Kate said that the doctor said they should still do a few more tests. The next slot isn't available for three weeks, at a time when Sara has to rush to a mountainside supply shop that specializes in natural building materials, but tiny ones. She learned about it after befriending niche dollhouse enthusiasts online. It's very specialized and somewhat secretive and is open only six hours a month. Kate is angry about going alone but Sara promises she will spend some of her bird nest money on a gift for her.

Thinking of names has become a new game. They can play over breakfast, before bed, while driving, walking. Anytime. It's a good distraction.

"Cora?" asks Sara.

"Is she going to be born eighty?"

"No. Sorry."

"I thought we had it narrowed down to our top five for each sex."

"Oh, I didn't know Alana was still in the mix."

"Well, it is. Although our baby is going to be so cool it won't matter if she's called Assface."

"I think it will."

"Oh, Sar, you're so practical. I mostly love that about you."

"I love you too."

Sara meets with May on the park bench near the tree. Their designated client meeting spot.

"I've been studying their nests. There was even an old one near my place. The architecture of them is fascinating," Sara says.

"Remember, the individual bird is important to study, too. This is not merely technical."

The bird tends to her empty nest or, at least, that's what it looks like. Sara is still not sure about the intricacies of finch behaviour, let alone this particular finch, who seems to have an intimate relationship with a very wealthy woman. She makes a mental note to read more about behaviour. When they bob their heads they could be saying no. They could be acting out some important drama. She's never worked so hard on something, never been more intrigued, confounded, pushed to understand the creature that will live in her invention.

"Sara!"

Eyes trained on a finch video on her iPad, she looks up at Kate, her narrow shoulders drenched in spring rain. A striped straw protrudes from her lips. A jumbo milkshake. A bad omen. In the corner of her lip, a bit of liquidy chocolate ice cream pools and sputters. Then Kate is on the kitchen tiles, her body limp and shapeless.

The doctor wasn't even going to try, she told Sara. There was no point. Her uterus was being an asshole, she said. Basically, her body hated babies, and they were not allowed to live in there.

"I shouted that I wanted to burn my body down! Then they gave me an Ativan."

None of her other doctors had ever mentioned that she had an inhospitable body cavity. Why had she assumed? Why had she let this dream go on without being prepared?

"I'm sorry I wasn't there."

"You were working. You can't be everywhere."

"I probably could have taken an hour."

"It doesn't matter where you are. My uterus is an asshole."

For the next week Sara keeps Kate comfortable. Camped

out on the armchair, her body curled away from the television, the window, trained on the corner of the room. Sara knows she imagined feeding the baby there, little fruit of her loins at her breast. Everything she can do to stop her from weeping, she does. Trips to the store result in bags of candy and chips, prescription meds, and Victoria Gin. She wraps Kate in blankets, threads pillows around her slouched form.

When Sara had asked about adoption, Kate had accused her of being unsympathetic. Had shouted and thrown her gin and ginger to the ground.

"You need to go to the doctor," Kate said. "You need to have your innards explored. You need to make a little Sara for me to love."

Every day after work, Sara meets May in the park. These meetings to sit and observe together. The first few tries, the nests are terrible. Sara knows this, and yet after her sixth she wants to present something to May, show her that she's been working hard on this project, that she's paid attention. In a small cake box from the bakery she's packed the nest in gold-flecked tissue paper, thinking it makes the structure and tones of the nest stand out. May's face remains stern as ever. She merely hands the box back.

"Please try again. I do appreciate the work you're doing."

They sit in silence, side by side on a bench, the same one they sat upon on the day they first met. May's breathing is calm and steady. Everything about her is so focused. The bird appears like it is willed by May. The only time her face softens is when the bird comes close to her, lands right on the knee of her designer jeans.

When the bird is near May, then Sara can take a closer look at them both. May's posture is less perfect than she originally thought. May's eyeliner is always thin and smooth. She favours neutral tones, except for her lip colours, which vary and are always vibrant. She is stern, but while the bird hops on her leg, looks up at May, her mouth cracks open slightly, feathers of a smile along the edges of her lips. For what seems like an hour, the bird happily enjoys May's leg as a perch. Then the bird trills a small song, as if she's asking May a question. In response, May reaches a small hand down, almost in slow motion she's so careful, and strokes the top of the bird's head. Usually so energetic, the bird remains still, petted like a content cat on a lap.

Sara fights her impulse to reach out and touch the bird herself, slip her hand flush with May's thigh.

Loud jazzy notes burst from Sara's pocket, her brassy ringtone for Kate, and the bird flies off instantly. May looks away in the direction of the bird.

"I'm sorry," Sara says, but May's gaze stays focused on the trees, doesn't acknowledge the apology.

Sara answers, hears Kate's agitated voice asking for more Reese's Peanut Butter Cups and gin, and muffles the call as she hurries over to a different bench to talk.

"I can't be at your beck and call. I'm working."

"Oh shit. Sorry. I thought I was your wife."

The light never goes out in her tiny garage studio. The light is always out in the house. They mostly communicate by phone, if they communicate at all. A text about toilet paper. Sara can see Kate sometimes in the light of the television, which Kate leaves on for company, though she doesn't pay attention to the exploits of Real Housewives. Sara has built a human nest out of sweaters and blankets, out of new pillows she bought herself. She never has to leave the studio, can work and sleep and dream all in one place.

Sara sneaks into the kitchen in the middle of the night for a snack. Kate has been sitting in the dark living room and shouts into the dark kitchen.

"God, this woman must be fucking special. You spend so much time with her."

Sara doesn't respond, spoons soup into her mouth, and stares at the curves of her bowl. A tight nest looks indestructible. They're designed to keep the eggs protected, encased. Everything reminds her of how this project seems to be failing.

She can't deny that she is intrigued by May. This woman who seemed so strange and unfathomable has elements to her, depth that Sara can't resist experiencing, even for brief moments in the wind-whipped park. Underneath the tree, May becomes more elegant than a yuppie in a gilded home.

"Are you ever going to come home again?"

"You're the one who told me to take the project!"

"I told you to do it for us. And this fucking baby that doesn't exist."

Sara doesn't know what to do. She plugs in her iPod, blasts noise, and walks back to her studio.

When she finally presents the finished nest to May, there is no fancy paper, though Sara did have to build a small stick structure to transport it safely. They meet in the park, as always. This time, May's face changes immediately. Not quite a smile but a flush of approval. She briefly holds the nest in her hands, then passes it back to Sara, gets a tissue from her purse, and dabs at her eyes.

"If this doesn't work, nothing will," May says.

"I really hope it does."

She's hired some men who work with movie actor animals to capture her bird, bring it to her gorgeously appointed home filled with expensive furniture, art, all the neutral clothes a closet can hold.

"I'm nervous," May says.

The bird is in her usual spot, neck jittering from side to side, so unaware of what is about to change. May watches her, clamps a hand on Sara's shoulder, a tight grip on her now tense body.

"Do you want to see where I'll be installing it?" she asks Sara.

Sara watches the bird take off and land softly on their usual bench.

"I'm too nervous."

Sara gets the call from May as she hauls a hamster mansion

to a townhouse in Coal Harbour. At first, the bird refused to leave her perch near the skylight, onyx pin eyes trained on the sky as it changed from day to night. After a few days of sorrowful singing, May trying her best to be accommodating like a tree, like a shrub, like a cloud, a puff of air, the bird soars in the loft, rounds the space, and finally lands in her nest. May watched to see if she would react. All through her trials, Sara had imagined the bird would reject it, tear each slim piece apart until the binder failed, and the whole structure would disintegrate, would disappear like dust fading into sunlight. Instead the bird rested.

"I am so grateful," May says.

In the background, Sara thinks she hears the short trill the bird makes when she's near May. No eggs to protect, no outside air, no tall trees or dirt. No manufactured bench, all of them sitting in silence, waiting for a meaningful moment. Sara isn't sure how to feel. But she's made her client happy. May is overjoyed.

The house is dark and quiet, no sign that anyone lives there, that two people used to share small touches as they passed each other on the staircase. Sara stares at the front door, considers knocking. Inside, it's confirmed. Kate is gone. Dishes in cupboards, no crumbs on the counter, throw pillows fluffed and perfect in the elbows of the couch. Nothing comfortable about this emptiness. Sara leaves through the back door, skirts the space in the drive where Kate's car should be. In her studio, she doesn't turn on the light. No work to be done. She coils herself into the blankets and sweaters. Her failed nests surround her as she hums a song she imagines a different kind of bird might sing.

Sometimes We Can Be That Way

Before the party, Phil waits for Karen, watches a puma tear into a deer in high-definition. She walks in front of the TV wearing a dress in the royal blue colour he once said made her eyes look sky clear.

"How do I look?" she asks, swirls the skirt to expose her thighs.

"Fine," he says and swishes his arm to remove her from his view. She backs up, and his eyes refocus on blood and fur.

She's not sure if he even registered that she's wearing clothes at all, or if it would matter if she isn't. In the closet, she holds hangers to her chest, drapes dresses and skirts over her frame. All the clothes on her side face toward her; his wardrobe hangs the other way. Backs of shirts ignore her. Stiff seams, closed buttons. She changes into a black skirt and top just before they leave. If she tries to use colour they'll be late.

After they moved in together, she changed the sheets once a week and cancelled her subscription to *Cosmo*. Weekends felt less desperate. Her desire for a small dog vanished. When someone called to tell her she'd been promoted, he gripped her shoulders and shook her with joy. He filled the other half of her closet with his buttoned shirts and tailored blazers. Their clothes looked beautiful together.

Her company gathers at a mid-range hotel to celebrate an unexpected victory. Girls in unfashionable vests glide past her with palm-sized napkins and finger-sized morsels, legs pumping to get back to the kitchen once their trays are emptied. Drinks are ordered from the velvet and oak bar across the room, where Phil holds the hand of a stranger, grips it and pumps, his best handshake. This is how he shows off, proves he is the manliest, most dedicated husband. Her co-workers love him at these events because he never intimidates as he mines the room for attention and gives a good amount in return. At home, his attention is always somewhere else.

Someone hands Karen a neat Scotch as she stands in a circle with her boss and his favourites. All she wants is to feel a light buzz. They clink glasses, down their thimblefuls of booze. It's not enough to make her easy. Celebrations feel like work. Eye contact that doesn't look forced, head nods slotted in without appearing like she's lost, conversations about TV personalities she's never heard of that don't result in awkward pauses. Often when she lingers, stares, she wonders if she looks as though she needs to have a quick nap.

At the bar she gets a double. The straw stabs her in the nose. She's distracted by watching Phil across the room, the way he talks to other people, pays attention, seems invested in their words and lives. Hands flail as he talks to her assistant, rapt by some story he'll claim later to be too tired to tell her. She stalks along the wall toward them, hides behind a leafy plant, listens and sips. Her all black clothes a fine choice for subtle spying, gathering intel on Party Phil. Get an idea of why he finds other people so fascinating.

He tells her assistant about how he works from home, his rules for self-motivation: make schedules and stick to them, prime yourself with a daily pre-dawn run, visualize end results with vivid details, make up a theme song about your self-worth and sing it whenever you're deterred. Laughing at this, she chokes on her drink, sputters. She's never heard him sing a personal theme song.

They must hear her. Phil pushes the leaves aside, reveals Karen crouched behind the dirty pot, a straw dangling from her lips, tears in her eyes. She stumbles out from behind the green fronds.

Karen can't stop laughing, has to sit on the edge of the planter, wipe her hands across her eyes and cheeks to sop up the tears. When her assistant asks what's so funny, she just keeps laughing because she doesn't know if she's laughing at him or herself.

"He does have a regimented schedule. It's called *TV Guide*," she says.

"I just like to learn, Karen. It's not like I'm screwing around all day. I don't even subscribe anymore. It's all online."

They must still have a subscription. He might as well highlight the pages, put reminders in his phone, weekly pings to rouse him to the couch for another episode of *Deadliest Science*

Fair Projects, or whatever it is he watches. Half his day is spent watching wildlife, space shuttles, guys with goggles proving each other wrong. His office is cluttered with stacks of papers fanned with sticky notes and an entire year of unread magazines. And yet he couldn't answer Karen two weeks ago as to when was the last time the two of them ventured out of the house for more than a trip to the grocery store.

"Karen?"

"Whatever. It's your thing. It's fine," she says.

Fine. It's fine, she thinks, bites her straw. Fine. Fine is not a fine word, and no one should use it to refer to another person's appearance. She slurps up cool fizz and alcohol. Karen's assistant looks at her as if she's been slashed with the shards of a broken bottle.

"What?" Karen asks.

"Your nose, there's blood."

With the back of her hand she swabs at her nostril, and a red smear appears on her skin. Eyes wide and crossed, her assistant excuses herself, says she has to make a phone call. Phil watches Karen struggle in her purse for a tissue. There isn't one. She tries to catch his eye, but he's staring at her bloody nose. He motions that he's heading to the bar. Her gnarled straw protrudes from the cubes of melting ice mingling with crimson drops. One of the vest-girls spins past, and Karen chases after her to abandon her glass on the empty tray.

In the bathroom mirror, she examines herself, her wounded nose, her simple black clothes. She notices rosy pops on her lips, must have drank some of her own blood. She dabs at the colour with balled-up toilet paper, then swipes hard until she can't tell it was ever there.

On her way back to the fray, she nearly barrels into Phil. He eats a breaded shrimp, turns to her. Mouth full, he doesn't speak, holds up another breaded shrimp. When she takes it from his hand, their skin doesn't touch. The deep-fried keeps them apart. She chews the warm hors d'oeuvre and thinks of the late dinner of snacks they ate so many years ago. When they both wanted to impress each other. After her car broke down, unfixable, on their first date. They got deep fried things to go, crispy golden food in little cardboard buckets that they ate in his bed. Each morsel tasted tender and sweet and full of old school sleepover comfort. With his hand, he'd fed her a piping hot onion ring, wiped hot sauce from her chin with his thumb, licked off her mess. After she swallowed the shrimp, she wanted to take his hand, put pressure on it with her fingers. She didn't.

Before she met him, life was sloppy because she liked herself but not really anyone else. Being a pair righted her, and she didn't apologize for it. Now they are like frayed socks that don't ball up neatly together, elastic shredded.

At home, Phil's forced to stare at Karen's ass while he fixes her broken zipper. Once she's unzipped and in bed, lights out, she sees him in silhouette as he folds his clothes and sets them on the dresser.

"Good night," he says to their dark room.

"Thank you," she says, but he's closed the door.

She hears the television, and sometimes there are cheers, and sometimes people are laughing. This is how she falls asleep, listening to the real joy and fake amusement through the speakers they picked out together. When he comes to bed he's groggy. He pulls at the covers and builds a wall with half the pillows, as though protecting himself against her.

She wakes in the middle of the night and pushes the rest of the pillows toward him, piles blankets on, makes him look comfortable enough to sleep on. Ear pressed to the cotton wall, she can't get shrimp out of her head, can hear him crunch the breaded coating, see him grin as if he'd caught the shrimp himself.

Before they were together, creaks in the night woke her. Wind in the folds of the curtain made her juvenile. After they met, she wanted to be a grown-up. He would put her coat on at the end of a meal and hold the restaurant door open. She would whisper in his ear and wrap her arm around him in the cab. She would massage every inch of his body, and he would thank her over and over until they were both asleep. But small thrills are gone, deep-fried holds no power. Memories are tricky and rude. Being a grown-up is full of paperwork and saying fine and cars that work properly almost all the time. On the other side of the pillow wall, he is gentle as a deer, sleeping vulnerable beside her.

In the grim grit of too early morning, she pushes herself into this puffy pile of linens, puts the whole weight of herself against it as though she must tear through and get to the other side. Karen's body pushes and won't stop pushing. She braces her legs on the floor and keeps pushing, until she's shoved the mass of everything on the bed onto the floor, including Phil. Karen's breathing as if she's been running hard, in pants and gulps. When she hears the thump of his body hitting the low pile carpet, she feels satisfied. Phil groans.

She crawls onto the bed, props her hands up under her chin, and smiles down at the heap of Phil and their bedding and giggles at the possibility of what will happen next.

Sleep Talk

"*Uhnnn.*"

I pull the sheets up high and try not to listen.

"*Again!*"

Sunbeams bump up against my eyelids.

"Mommy's got a marigold."

I vow to rip out the flowers along the patio.

"*Uhnnn.*"

His morning breath burns my earlobe.

"Marigolds! *Ha, ha, ha!*"

I haul myself out of bed and wince at the coldness of the floor. The sun is up, but it's still chilly out and too early to be climbing around the house trying to function. Some people love spring mornings, but I hate them. Everything is just coming awake and too little and too fresh and too unlike me in the morning, except for my husband, who is sleeping and is not fresh or little but very loud in his sleep and regular size.

Back when we first got married, Mitch didn't even mumble in his sleep. Little snorts here and there, maybe a sigh, but no words, no phrases, no sentences. Even a year ago, it was just a loud exhale if anything at all, nothing like this. Nothing loud enough to wake me up several times in the course of a night.

His midlife crisis must be occurring in his sleep.

I force my eyes to stay open wide as I shower. I could easily fall asleep standing up like a withered old nag while the conditioner burns a hole in my cornea. I press my ear to the bathtub wall and hear him laughing about the little orange petals.

I peek in on him before heading downstairs. Our bedroom is quiet now, and his hand is groping for the empty space where I'm supposed to be sleeping. Marigolds were the first thing we planted when we bought this house. It's funny to think that he even remembers. I blow him a kiss.

Somewhat weary, I head out early to run errands. I picture Mitch and Ween having father-daughter time over sugary cereal and healthy omelettes. They never complain that I can't cook. Keeping their lives organized and clean seems to suit them just fine. The note I've taped to the kitchen table isn't nagging. *Hey guys, I fixed Ween's backpack—it's on the desk. Don't forget to lock the back door again! Mitch, doctor at 3. Dinner at 6 (I'll get Chinese?) because Dad's curling (2nd night this week!). No one eat the candy I bought for Grandma!!* I always punctuate with an xoxoxo.

When I get to work the copy machine is broken, and everyone is crowded around it. I join in because I'm too tired to think about mortgages. We all stare too long and too hard, and I feel my eyelids quiver. Someone notices.

"Tara, coffee?"

I nod my head yes, not even knowing who I'm speaking to but grateful that someone is going to give me a boost this morning. I take the cup without acknowledging who my caffeine saviour is and then pour back some scalding gulps. This day will turn out to be okay.

"Again?"

Mitch is wearing oven mitts. He questions me about his nighttime behaviour as though I have answers. Strands of Ween's long wet hair lace my fingers as I pull them into a braid, while she gets our advice on science fair projects. The kitchen table is full of books I checked out of the library.

"Yes. It was pretty loud. The loudest you've ever been in your sleep," I say.

"I didn't hear anything. What about crystals?"

"Crystals? Get real, kid. What about something with explosions?"

The braid is too loose, so I take it apart and start again.

"Something about flowers."

Ween jerks her head around in shock. "Mom. Flowers are lame."

I turn her head back to face her homework and point to a book about rockets. I twist her hair into a bun and wrap a checkered hair tie around it. "I was talking to Dad, Janine. Flowers. You were very into marigolds."

"That's weird. I'll try to keep it down. Somehow," Mitch says.

"Dad's right. Explosions are the way to go."

The timer goes off, and Mitch turns to the oven. The aroma

of confetti cupcakes fully distracts Ween from explosions and flowers. When she jumps up to take one from the tins, her loose bun opens, and wet hair slaps her back. "I wanted a braid, Mom."

We decorate the warm cupcakes at the table, careful not to drip icing on the library books. Ween forces Mitch to take the ones she did to his curling team. I walk him to the car, his arm around my waist.

"Honey, draft beer and cupcakes?" I ask.

"Once they've had enough beer, they won't be thinking about food and beverage pairings."

I give him the guilt look, but he kisses me over and over, on the mouth, on the cheek, on the neck, one hand resting on the open car door, the other on the small of my back.

"Please?" he says.

I take the cupcakes back inside and hide them in the coat closet until Ween goes to bed.

Bursting out from under the duvet, I struggle to find the alarm clock. Blue spots dangle in front of my face—I must have bolted up too fast. When they fade, I realize I have only been asleep for one hour. Mitch has snuck into bed sometime during that time.

"Whisky sour and a Strongbow."

His mouth makes different shapes when he talks in his sleep. The vowels are too open, and the rest is a slur. I've tried shaking and kicking and biting, but Mitch is comatose when he's chatty. I pinch his nose tight with my fingers and cup his mouth, a technique my brothers liked to use on our dog when he would snore. Just like that dog, Mitch snorts snot onto my fingertips, nips my palm, and turns over. I wipe my hand on my nightgown.

"Oh, Julie."

My feet hit the floor as Mitch exhales this name. Feet stuck to the carpet fibres like flypaper, I hold my breath. Staying still, I wait for him to confirm the name, or say another one, throw some other characters into the mix, have a dream conversation with a Ted or a Dr. Heller. I don't think I know any Julie. Or maybe he said something else, and I'm too worn to pick up on it. Without regular sleep, words don't resemble real communication.

"*No!*"

He pushes his pillow out of the bed, and just like that old dog, Mitch twitches his dream out. I pad down the hall in my robe, tripping on the belt.

"Honey? Weenie? Mama's going to crash with you tonight, okay?"

Ween doesn't budge. I don't have the power to wake anyone up. I shift her over onto the other side of the bed. If only we'd bought her that bunk bed she wanted so badly, then I would have an alternative. The warmth from her body is lovely. A light rain taps gently on her window, and when I look outside there is the smooth dark blue of night. Ween's room is a sleep refuge.

"Oh, yes! *Yes! Fuck yes!*"

I turn over and hope this is all in my own dreams.

"You ... are ... so ... hot!" Mitch pants in spurts.

Before I run down the hall, I make sure that Ween is still sound asleep. I need to get there to shut him up, but trying not to wake her makes me slow.

"Dirty, barnburning *fuck!*"

I stand in the hallway waiting for more, but he's done for now, so I crawl back in beside Ween, carefully pull her hair into even segments and braid it tightly.

Polly likes to talk about everything and anyone. She is my favourite and least favourite gossip. Lunches are never boring, although I'm concerned that my current state of mild confusion might make this conversation like an acid flashback. Too bad I didn't drop any acid back when I was less uptight. I probably wouldn't know much about anything trivial or scandalous if it wasn't for Polly. Today there is no pleasant banter; we're straight into the deep stuff before I have time to fully peel the plastic wrap off the sandwich Mitch made me.

"Mike's dick is partially inside his stomach. And it's been like that forever, but his parents thought it would just drop on its own because they were Jehovah's Witness or something and didn't think that it would be a problem. But now it is, and he has this new girlfriend, who is young and very stupid, and basically he has to either be a bachelor forever or have some crazy operation."

"Mike from upstairs, or Mike the janitor?" I brush the crust of my sandwich against my lips and feel like I might be sick.

"And the company won't pay for the operation because they say that it's cosmetic, so he might just have to have a half-er forever."

"How did you get this information? About Mike ..."

"From upstairs. Mike from upstairs. Tara! I'm wasting this story on you, Tara, I swear up and down his teeny cock."

There is a dollop of mayo oozing out onto my thumb, and the thinly sliced capicolla is rolled so tidily between the brown bread it couldn't look less appetizing. And the colours are all wrong. This penis talk is making me think too much. I wonder if I could just walk away and find a quiet place to nap.

"Anyway, the information came from Roberta, who gave him a down-the-pants jobbie at the Christmas party two years ago, and it was ridiculously small and weird, and so she asked, and he told her the whole story. Cried in her cleavage."

The uneaten sandwich looks like I imagine a fart to look if farts weren't made of gas, and I dry heave big and bold.

"That's disgusting."

"Sorry, Polly."

I settle down, glad that nothing actually came up. Polly is furiously eating her beet salad, staining her mouth a charming shade.

"Were they both drunk at the time?" I am trying hard to remember if I was at that party.

"God, fucking mercy, Tara, of course they were drunk. That's how I know it's all true. Mike had the elixir of truth in his system, and Roberta got the goods right out of him."

"How was your day at work, babe?"

Mitch works in an office. There are fluorescent lights and other people that work around him. He tells blue collar people what to do, and sometimes he fires them. We usually don't talk about work at home. That's for what we call "Living Time." It creeps into our lives when we leave the house during the day, but no need to know too much about work. Work is how we make money to buy handmade wood furniture and special gifts for each other, just because. Work is for making new acquaintances and talking about work-related things and work-related stress. Home is for keeping house and relaxing and delicious meals and love. Or that is what it's supposed to be.

Instead of lying to Mitch or confronting him again in the broad evening light, I just grab him and press my face into his chest and inhale, not knowing whether or not someone else has pressed her face into this shirt. He still smells like our laundry detergent, the pine scent strengthened by the needles that sometimes blow on to the fresh laundry when I set the basket near our open bedroom window. He still smells like someone who lives here and wears clothes that are washed and folded by his wife.

"I missed you. You weren't in bed last night. Was I talking in my sleep again?"

"Yes."

"What did I say?"

Hiding the fear in my eyes is as necessary as looking directly into his. "Nothing interesting."

Four nights in a row, Mitch belts out Julie's name and different sexual iterations of pleasure.

"Bandolier banging!"

"Julie!"

"Gonna bust that box!"

"My Julie."

"Sweet, fragrant, marigold muff!"

"Julie! Julie! Julie!"

The flower metaphor. That's when it stung. She must be a
redhead. Julie. My whole body bloomed into anger, like those
prickly purple flowers atop those even pricklier weeds.

Turned up as loud as it goes, the speakers are still terrible, but I
don't think that's the problem. I had rigged my old Dictaphone
from college to record Mitch's murmurings, thinking I'd be better at analyzing them when it isn't two a.m., and I'm not jarred
awake. I slept on the couch, let the sound of Ron Popeil lull me
to sleep, and woke up fairly rested. The sounds it recorded are
vague and wispy. I thought to put it under the mattress on my
side of the bed so he wouldn't see it, but all I can hear is the rustle
of sheets and the creaky moans of the box spring.

Mitch and I just let things go. As long as my note is obeyed,
I don't care if he wants to curl three nights a week or go for a
drink after work. There is a schedule, and it works, and I write

it on a piece of graph paper every morning. And right now there is something that is not on the graph paper, and I don't know what it is.

Mitch loves to curl. A dreary game made drearier by the bad lighting and poor quality vodka in their Black Russians. He has three games a week and a bonspiel. He likes to think he's one of the guys. I hate it and stay home to watch bad TV with Ween. We've only been twice. But have we ever been invited? When Polly finally notices that I'm out of sorts, she stops talking about Jen Vanelli's addiction to prescription inhalers.

"This is good shit, and you're acting like we're talking world events. What are you thinking about?"

"Curling."

"Curling?"

"I'm not sleeping much."

Polly convinced me to eat outside today, even though the wind keeps whipping our paper napkins off the bench. Her salad of choice today is covered in creamy dressing and bacon bits.

"So you're not sleeping much and thinking about curling."

The bonspiel runs the whole weekend. Three days of drinking and rocks and fleece jackets and hurry hard. And I'm going.

"That husband of yours curls?"

I nod. Polly offers me some bacon bits, but I don't respond.

"All right. Why aren't you sleeping?"

"Mitch yells in his sleep."

"Really?"

Polly is fascinated. Her eyes pop, and she clutches her salad container to her chest. The wheels in her head are turning, and I can only hope they'll also help me. I don't even care that this will become Polly's lunchtime conversation with someone else on a different bench tomorrow.

"About another woman."

"Well, this is something to think about."

Ween and I are packed into the plastic seats with the other wives. Some of them don't even know who we are, two strangers watching the final bonspiel of the year. Mitch doesn't know we're here. Ween is thrilled that we are and that it is a surprise for her dad. I feel like an undercover agent.

I don't see Mitch anywhere, but my view is limited. There are curlers drinking and laughing and spilling coffee in every corner. His rink's not supposed to be on the ice for another hour, but he's been out of the house for two. I thought I'd find him bonding with his buddies at the bar, throwing down a few mid-morning drafts.

"I should have made a sign for Dad."

Most of the women are seated with us. Slouching and supportive, aging, bleached-out former beauties wearing tank tops, teen daughters checking their nails, curling rink grannies with curling rink sweatshirts. A cross section of women I can't imagine Mitch having anything to do with. I scour the crowd to see if there is anyone worth my time.

"Why didn't we make a sign? Or a shirt like that lady's?"

There are a few younger women on a couch by the fireplace, sipping coffee and lacing up their curling shoes. A group of younger men is standing around them, pouring from a flask into their mugs.

"Mom!"

Ween whacks me in the arm.

"Look at that lady's shirt. God."

Ween points at the woman sitting next to us. It's one of the grannies, sporting the name of Mitch's rink on her chest. She's done it in gold and red glitter paint, cut out photos of the team ironed on the front and back. I can't help that it makes me uncomfortable. Her energy is huge, and she jumps up out of her chair. The excitement of my plan wanes when I see Mitch slide out to his team. His reaction is disheartening. The smile on his face is enormous as he taps a teammate and points up at us. His happy waving proves nothing. If he'd been surprised to see her, had stumbled on the ice, that would be a sign that something was up.

"That's my grandson out there. Who's yours?"

"That one. The one smiling and waving."

"That's nice. Haven't seen you here before."

I dread having to stay for the entire game, the entire weekend.

"Look at Dad! The surprise worked, Mom."

Another terrible night. It doesn't matter where I sleep; these thoughts, his shouts, they find me on the couch, in Ween's room, in the basement. The sounds have transitioned. Mitch's nightly content is more like his waking conversation. It's domestic and devoted.

"I love you."

"Muffin, you can do this."

"Sure, your mom's place on Sunday."

"I love roast!"

I get up at night and Google. Too many Julies in the world. I try Facebook. No Julies connected to Mitch or me. She could have a hidden profile. She could be lying about her boring name. I try thinking about every woman I've ever met in town. I can't think. I can't sleep. I don't even know if my brain is operating normally, or if at this point I'm making up a whole mess of stories in my head because of the not sleeping and not thinking.

For a minute it's quiet, me sitting at the kitchen table in the morning, and then happy feet hit the stairs.

"Good morning, Tara." He ruffles his own hair while reaching out to me from the kitchen doorway. I've poured him a fresh cup of coffee, which is sitting patiently on the counter.

"Thanks for coming to the bonspiel."

"Beer's in the fridge."

He opens the door and pulls out the milk.

"It's seven a.m."

"Milk, eggs, juice, fruits are in the fridge."

Mitch rests his coffee mug on my shoulder. He doesn't remove it, so I look up at him and see that he's smiling down on me. My face is too tired to say anything. I dip my head forward, and the towel wrapped around my hair falls into my oatmeal. Mitch grabs a dirty dishcloth and swipes at the goo. I take another spoonful before throwing my head back, and the oatmeal towel splats to the floor.

Thankfully, I don't offer Ween a beer when she marches down the stairs. Mitch has made her snowman-shaped pancakes by dropping three little ones side by side on the pan. At nine she still falls for it. My own child is a total idiot, and I know she got her gullibility from me.

"Ween! Snowmen are up. Here's a bacon scarf." Mitch throws a jaunty piece of bacon on the pancakes and three chocolate chips for buttons.

"This snowman looks stupid."

Ween and Mitch stare at me, baffled by my comment. I kick my slippers out of the kitchen ahead of me and try to imagine how they can be so fucking chipper. Before I climb the stairs, I remember all the things I was supposed to remind Ween of in my regular daily note. Instead of going back to write it down, I just yell out a reminder for each stair.

"Lunch is in the fridge, add a banana. A page of your science homework is on the couch. Piano lessons at three-thirty. Come straight home. Dinner will not be takeout, so don't ask. Your father's putting stew in the slow cooker. Badminton practice is at seven."

By the top stair, my voice is shrill, and I take a moment to think about whether or not I sound like my mother. She never left notes.

I nap in my desk chair on my lunch break. The window is half open, and I dream that a bird flies into my sleeping mouth, and I choke. When I wake up, there are two dirty wrens looking at me from the telephone pole. They look evil, so I shut the window and try to get another ten minutes of REM.

"Tara!"

Squawks from the birds and Polly's voice combine in a force that begs not to be ignored. But I do anyway.

"Tara!"

I feel Polly's head hovering over me.

"Tara. You need to deal with this problem. Now. Look at you."

I know how I look. Rough. Tired. Beaten. And Polly is supposed to help me, not insult me. I squint my eyes tighter.

"Leave me alone." I shove my limp hand in the direction of Polly's face.

"Over the weekend, I did some thinking," she says.

"Polly. I don't want to hear about someone getting something edible stuck in one of their orifices and having to go to the emergency room and the doctor being some handsome guy she used to date in high school."

Polly pulls one of my eyes open with her fingers.

"Your problem. I was thinking about your problem. And by the way that story is one hundred percent accurate."

I don't want to think about my problem. I want to sleep in my office, keep my eyes shut, and imagine that I don't have a problem, that there is no mystery to be solved, because I don't have the power to solve it.

"Why don't you just talk to him?" she says.

"This is what you think of?"

Tears burn hot in the corners of my eyes. I crumple a stack of credit checks into my face.

"Well, you need to figure this out, or you're going to be an even bigger mess."

Polly puts her hand on my head, and I feel like I could explode into raging sobs. I don't want him to know that I know, that I suspect.

"Talk back. Get the truth out of him."

I've shipped Ween off to a sleepover on a school night and look like a very cool parent. I've set the table, and the wine is decanting. And if Mitch doesn't want the truth to come out with wine, he can have beer or Scotch, or a fine brandy or a wine cooler. It's all the same to me.

"Tara?"

My earlier outburst is my excuse for this meal, for Ween's sleepover. I take Mitch's coat at the door and lead him to the dining room.

"You didn't—"

"No, I didn't cook this."

I laugh at this brief display of naiveté, and we settle in for gourmet food and a few bottles of pinot noir.

I rub Mitch's feet after the meal, sitting on the couch

together with no TV, no music, just us. I've poured him a neat Scotch and slipped some brandy into his decaf espresso as well, both of which are sitting next to him on the coffee table. He's already drunk, and as I lull him to sleep with my thumbs on his instep I panic that maybe he only talks in bed, that he'll have a peaceful evening nap if he's in the living room.

"Honey, thank you." He slurs when he says this, just like in his sleep talk.

"Mitch. Shhh. Just relax."

I point to the Scotch, and he obeys, takes a hearty sip. I try to keep a rhythm with my massage, try to maintain my veneer of calm. His eyes close, and I wait. I smooth my hands over his feet and up his ankles and calves, and I wait. I wait until I hear the first mumbles of sleep, the loud exhale or satisfaction of being in his dream world. I'm not sure if I continue to wait for him to say something or jump right in.

"Fuck."

I'm not ready. It's like phone sex or dirty talk, things I've never done or am no good at.

"Yes ... Mitch."

His lips look swollen, like pepperoni, and are slick with saliva. During dinner, he sloshed wine onto his shirt, and now he's sweating through it. No need to be nervous around this man.

"Oh yes."

"Do you like that?"

I pluck at each toe to steady my voice.

"Oh, yes."

"Say my name, say I'm sexy."

He must recognize my voice. Even in his sleep, he must. But he doesn't. He slurs out this woman's name.

"You're sexy, Julie. So sexy."

He sounds like a child, words coming out of his mouth loose and sloppy.

"What about your wife?"

"What?"

"Your wife?"

"You're my wife, baby marigold."

I grab his big toes and squish them tight in my fists. Then I slide out from under his sleeping legs and up to bed. From there, I hear one last blast before I fall asleep.

"Now, suck 'em, Julie. Suck my toes."

It's the best I've slept in months. Ever since the first disruptive wake-up as Mitch shouted expletives. Coffee in my hand, I'm awake and I see. Mitch is the same as always. Jokes with Ween, ruffles his hair, is slyly sweet with me because he knows I'm creeped out by a more sickly affection.

But maybe Julie loves it. At night, Julie comes to him, his dream wife. And there she is, so loving, and she can do it. Marigold pubes, Julie there to dote and careen toward him in public spaces. Quiet in the stands, she watches him curl three nights a week. Maybe has her own homemade glitter shirt, a fleece that Mitch nuzzles into.

He never seems tired after his escapades. The courtship

of hot sex, the wedding that somehow I missed, the dinner at his mother-in-law's house, all the roast he seems to eat, the toe-sucking fetish that hopefully is only a sleep turn on. Maybe Julie will have a child. A little girl like Ween, but more Julie-like. Whatever that means.

I watch Mitch pack our lunches. Perfect baguettes full of carefully selected meat and cheese in our matching lunch bags. Ween grips his arm to try and sneak extra cookies into hers. This level of happiness is almost sickening. But it's good. And Julie is good. And we're all in this together.

Instructions for Having an Affair

Read this first:

Don't think it's as easy as going to some bar. It never is. That kind of thinking is what will cause disappointment.

Get Organized:

Details. That's what it's best to excel at. Like in an Excel spreadsheet. Keep track of things in Kodachrome code. Colours that correspond to fantasies, set to make reality.

Organize everything on the computer in secret documents. Filenames must be boring:

"Dessert Recipes"

"June Meeting"

"Raw Images"

And yet, they allude to something dirty or dangerous for you. Only you need to know the details. Only you need to know how to make yourself a wet mess. Even if it's just while looking at a few typed sentences on a black-and-white grid in a document on a desktop computer. The world might want us to be more elaborate than we want to be. Alleviate pressure by knowing your limit, by playing within it, by laying yourself out on your desk in the middle of the night and using an old joystick in ways that make you glad no one uses joysticks for playing video games anymore.

Communication:

"Honey." Still call your husband "Honey." If that's his nickname, that's the name you must use. Call him "Barracuda," or "Babe," or "Al," if that's his name, and you keep it serious, you keep it in the realm of the real without that added element of twee nuance. Not everyone needs it. But needs, that is what we're talking about. And yours are not being met in some way.

Figure this out. Answer questions. Do you hate the phrase oral pleasure, but your partner insists on using it? Are you sleepier than usual? Ask yourself: what is missing? Attention? Lust? The deep pull of emotion that used to rule your life and bring you joy? Find your own questions. Work with a deep integrity to answer them. Put them on the spreadsheet. Save the document with full knowledge that you are setting out to make your dreams come true.

Locations for Meetups:

The grocery store aisle with the most potential is the baking section. You can go homemade and shop to impress. Boxed cakes are surprisingly an aphrodisiac. There is something in their preservatives. The powder itself can function like mild cocaine. Draw lines on your hand and snort in the aisle. You will laugh and then feel like you can't take it anymore. This will cause hands to come together, mouths to breathe into each other.

Never waste your time in a coffee shop. Coffee culture is decidedly unsexy. No one is thinking about their bereft heart in a coffee shop. No one is thinking about anyone else's well-being in a coffee shop. If you want pastries and caffeine as a supplement for love, that's fine. Even encouraged. Do not misunderstand what it is. Because it is merely something that is unrelated to affairs.

Libraries are quiet, and people are often lonely. Leave your name in the search bar of the communal computer and your location in the stacks.

A park bench is a starting place. An art gallery too committal. A casino is a wonder, so loud and bright and full of potential.

Locations for Sex:
There are only "do nots" in the section. Do not think about your own home. If they are single, you may think about theirs but it must not be the only place. You will lose yourself. Not in a fun, wild, sexual way. In the way that causes you to forget to pick up children, to turn off your phone reminders, causes a small rash that develops into a small dragon that haunts you every time you try to have a shower. Fire-breathing, pocket-sized, the taunting and harassment only ceases when you're heartbroken.

Hotel and motel rooms are fine as anything. Alleys are fine too, if you're not squeamish. Hand sanitizer and Wet Ones are a great investment. Have them in your car or purse or backpack. Like a Boy Scout, you must be prepared even after you've left your spreadsheet hidden under domestic chores.

Off-season dugouts are good. Bring blankets. You are an adult. You own some things that will help make your life easier.

Practice levitating, and you can do it almost anywhere. Above the crowds. Bodies pressed in bliss.

Hollow out a large animal. This is not ideal, but once you try it, you'll be surprised how easy it is to desire it again and again.

This list could go on and on.

Locations for Emotional Outpourings:
This is best done in parked cars. There is no better place. Hidden on a side street. In a rooftop Best Buy parking lot. Parking garages are not ideal. The idea that someone could see you crying, yelling, confessing some other indiscretion to your already secret lover is essential. Fog up a window with feelings.

Anecdote:
I am only telling you this to make your experience more honest. The way it's gone for me has been like this.

I make a decision. To have an affair. I create worksheets for myself. I fill them out. I shred them. I fill them out again. I create spreadsheets. I fill them in.

My fantasies are big and bold. I want to teleport into my lover's bedroom, into their car, shrink down to the size of a cell and enter their body. I want to explore the inside of someone I love, and touch the tender vessels that make them breathe and walk, and stand in awe of the beauty of another person. I want flowers. I know they die. I still want them. I want someone to hold my hand and drag me to a dark corner in a public place.

Dark corners are not to be feared in an affair. This is where skirts are lifted, pants are unzipped, bodies crumpling together in pleasure and sorrow and minute moments of happiness.

None of this is revolutionary. Remember this.

I want to be loved and fucked. I want my partner to feel an unnamed shame. I want this person I committed to for life to question their own choices, to try to understand me like they used to, but to fail because we are more apart than ever.

I want so much to not feel like a monster. But I will. The tiny dragon is just like me. Judgmental and rude. I can't levitate or teleport. I can only make coffee for myself in the morning, no time to go to some café full of young people with time on their hands, with hope for the future, even for just the weekend. I can only ball up my fists and punch the laundry bag. I can only drive to work and cry as I sing the loudest to any song that comes on the radio, even if the lyrics are wrong. I can only remember the way I used to feel when my love first took my body and just held it, like I was a magical creature, something undiscovered and unlike anything else.

I write this down. I make another spreadsheet. I plan for the future.

Unplanned, I snapped to action in that moment I kissed

the mail carrier. We snuck into the mail truck and fucked like teens, sloppy and without finesse on other people's lives, letters, and bills. Then I walked. Forgetting everything else. Just for that day. Then I only remembered those minutes in the truck. Flashbacks. Flashes. Not magical.

Conclusion:

But don't mistake the level of dream fulfillment. It might not work out. You might come crawling back home with a fistful of greasy coins you didn't put into the gambling machine slots.

Full Price

Girls armed with plastic forks crowd around a chocolate pastry in the lunchroom. The air is filled with white sugar, cheap cocoa, and four different kinds of perfume. They spear cakey bits, swing them up to their lips and snap their teeth down around white forks smeared with saliva and doughiness. The brown paper bag with the round green logo, so familiar to Sam, is torn like a downed mouse after the hunt. The gooey insides gone, thin wrapper left dotted with brown flecks of cake.

Sam walks past them to the manager's office at the end of the narrow room. These girls have names that frequently appear on *Nancy Grace*, bold letters under her face, names that match up with new ticker tragedy. When she knocks on the open door, they toss their forks to the table. One of them looks up at her, still chewing her tiny morsel. One of them says her name and another echoes the syllable, fear in her voice. One of them balls the garbage up in her hand.

"Hi, girls," Sam says, waves less like a greeting than as a way of shooing away their liquid-bright eyes.

"How are you?"

"You look great."

"Sorry."

"Yeah, me too."

Still talking, they file out onto the sales floor. The store opens in fifteen minutes.

Sam wants to apologize for being late. She'd been able to wake up early every day before today, her first day back to work. When she'd had nothing to do but be a widow and count out how many Lean Cuisine dinners were left in the freezer, it had been easy to get out of bed. Last night had been her first bad night since the week of the accident. Each night for a week after the midnight call telling her Fred had tried to save the bank deposit, had lost, and had been pushed in front of a speeding SUV, she'd stayed up until the birds chirped, telling her she'd missed out on sleep. In their bed, she felt drowned by the sheets.

Jill sits in front of a frozen computer screen, her hand furiously moving the mouse over the surface of the desk. Sam knocks again. Jill slams the mouse against the arm of the chair.

"What?"

"Sorry, Jill. I'm late."

Jill looks over at Sam and smashes her head against the keyboard.

"God. I am so sorry. Sam. You're back." Her voice is muffled, her chin and lips clicking against the keys as she talks.

"It's okay."

"This place is a hellhole."

Jill gets up and moves to where Sam stands with her hands clasped against the zipper of her mid-rise jeans, name

236

tag already pinned to her striped pin-tucked blouse. Without warning, Jill crushes Sam against her chest. This is not like the hugs at the funeral, the hugs at the hospital, the hugs from her family so afraid to break her after she's already been broken. Sam hugs her back, and Jill pulls away. Looking down to avoid eye contact, Sam notices Jill's not wearing any shoes with her perfectly new, perfectly Gapified outfit. Medicated foot cream odor fills Sam's nose.

"We've missed you, babe. We've all been thinking about you."

Sam nods like a distracted child. She makes an effort to breathe through her mouth.

"Are you ready to get out there?"

"Yeah."

"There was supposed to be something here for you, but I thought you were back tomorrow. I'm a jerk. Did you get the flowers and basket we sent?"

"Yeah. Thanks."

"I know it probably didn't mean much, but we had to send something."

"Anything I should know about before I start my shift?"

"Sorry. It's terrible. So frigging terrible. We've got a promotion on polos."

The rest of the staff is huddled around the cash desk, listening to another manager, a new guy with bright eyes and slim trousers and an accusing look. He tells everyone what their goals are for the day and pushes the polo promotion, then sends staff off in all directions. They walk past Sam and smile, or pat her arm, or look away. Half of the cake girls will be stationed in the fitting room. Sam will be at the men's denim wall folding jeans into tight blue shapes.

"You're late," the new manager says.

"She's fine!" Jill yells from across the store.

"Sorry. I'm Sam. You're new."

"Not that new, honey," he says, bolts across the floor with his clipboard.

Sam pulls pairs of boot cuts out of their cubbyhole homes and presses them back together with the edges in rigid symmetry. On her right is a cube laden with pastel one-pocket T-shirts. She leans over and breathes in their fresh Styrofoam chip scent. To her left is the khaki wall, a totally different fold, shape, wear. A completely different kind of man wears khakis. Fred wore khakis. Even before they were married, even before they'd kissed under the snowy fibreglass ceiling of the mall parkade on a rainy winter morning, he'd worn khakis. It was part of his job, but he also liked the way they fit, the neutrality of them.

He managed a Starbucks on street level, and she worked on the lower level of the mall, underneath that Starbucks. He was the same height as her and had a crop of wheaten curls on his head, a supple chocolate leather belt around his waist, and a polite stutter. Before her shift, she'd order a Tall, to go. He knew her order, and by the time she was at the front of the line it would be ready to go, cardboard sleeve nestled around the cup. She would notice when his curls were taking over his head and usually a day or two later would be complimenting him on a new haircut.

One day he gifted her a travel mug, leftover and green with snowflakes from the Christmas line. He admitted when he handed it to her, full of steaming Gold Coast blend, that it was on sale, no big deal, but thought she looked like the kind of person who would use a travel mug if she had one around. His honesty was charming, the way he put himself out there, but not too hard, not by spending full price. She imagines the cake girls would laugh at someone buying them a gift for less than the original retail price, tossing it to the ground in a dramatic attempt to break it and the giver's heart.

After that, the baristas had looked at her funny when she walked in and set her shiny travel mug on the counter to be filled. She couldn't tell if they thought she was weird or if they were jealous. They all seemed protective of him, and yet, none of them had snatched him up, taken him home after a late shift, coaxed him onto their futon couches, and made him a husband. Sam wasn't scared to take him home, to wait for him in the parkade that night, and let him know she wasn't headed to her own car. Sitting shotgun, she tapped her foot impatiently. His car smelled of takeout containers and cherry air freshener and him. Dark roast and hair gel and Right Guard and ocean. Permanent on his skin, a salty, tingly aroma.

From where she's stationed, Sam can see two of the girls admiring themselves in the fitting room mirrors. They poke at their abdomens with willowy fingers, can almost wrap their hands around their neck-thin waists. Sam can't believe that the four of them are satisfied with sharing a measly pastry. She used to eat a pastry every day. When she worked the morning shift, she went before work. If she worked a mid, then after the lunch rush, when she got to take her break. On the late shift, she'd wait until after closing, get one to go. At home in her pyjamas, with the TV far too loud, she'd sink her teeth into an oat fudge bar, or a coffee cake, or a plastic-wrapped slice of banana bread. She always hoped he'd be at the bar. And most of the time he was. Fred never gave her free pastries. He was a stickler for the rules.

Being a young widow is a strange burden, carries nostalgia that she isn't sure she wants. She's a working widow, punished by cotton socks and perfect folded jeans. There had been no time to stay at home. The bills were piling up, the modern-day retail romance over. The mall dream had died, and so had Fred, and Sam had to go back to telling older women to go up a size without also telling them their legs aren't sausages.

Sam wanders the men's section, runs her hands over the chilled cotton of the shirts and shorts, the brightness of everything. She helps a man pick out cargo shorts and a woman find a buttoned shirt in the right plaid for her husband. From the fitting room, the cake girls come and tell her to switch out. They go the front of the store, stand by the window, and watch for cute guys coming in.

When she gets to her new post, there are women waiting

for different sizes, a man trying to roll a cuff on a pair of jeans that are too long for him, another fighting with the lock on his door. There are rumpled clothes on the floor that she picks up and piles on a shelf. Sam calls the new manager for sizes in trousers and a blouse. He shows up a minute later, shoves the hangers into her chest, snorts, and throws his hands across his clipboard. Sam knows he's watching, making sure she does all the sales steps. After she compliments the women and curls a perfect roll on the bottom of the man's jeans, Sam looks up and the new manager is gone. The guy with the lock problem emerges and explains why each piece isn't right for him as he hands them to her. He is so apologetic it makes Sam's chest burn. In the corner of the fitting room she takes deep whiffs of the shirts as she folds them, inhales the scent of every man who's tried on a new look. One of them must have a flake of comfort or pain or remembrance.

After two hours of folding, she's called to the cash desk. Someone is taking lunch, and she needs to be refreshed on cash procedures.

"Since I hear that was where you worked before," says the new manager. "Don't forget. Polos."

In the enclosed square of the cash desk, she tidies up stray tags, moves hangers into their correct bins. She sells a family of jeans to a woman with a torn purse. The cake girls beg Jill to switch their breaks so that they can take their lunches two by two. She slams open the lunchroom door, and two of them skip through it together. Sam would hate to have that job.

There have been positions open, but she can't imagine dealing with employees like they're her children. She is the kind of person who likes having someone else in control. Looking pained, Jill splits up the other two girls, and they slouch off in different directions. She walks over to Sam, grips the desk, and leans back for a stretch.

"Sam, did you see these new scents? Some of them don't even smell that bad. Remember Midnight Tango?"

"Sadly, I do."

Jill holds the round bottles under Sam's nose for her to test. One peachy, another more citrus, one spicy, one too woody, and it makes her back away. Another stings her nostril, a hint of alcohol, but mostly a breezy, saline ocean smell.

"Nice, huh?"

Sam nods and puts a hand up to her eyes. Through the glisten at the start of tears, she sees a woman with a stroller roll up to the desk. Jill swoops up the bottles and arranges them back into a display. Sam moves without thinking, passes barcodes over the scanner. The scent sinks into her, embeds itself in her head, waves through her skin. In two weeks they would have been married for six months. In six weeks, Sam will be twenty-three.

When she looks up from the till, the woman and baby are gone. The new manager glares at her over top of his clipboard. Another woman piles camisoles on the desk.

"Did you know that all polos are eighteen-fifty? All colours, men's and women's."

Sam chokes through the spiel, points at the tables laden with vibrant shirts. The bottles of eau de toilette are two feet away. Smells sell. During a staff meeting, that's what someone had said, that people are more likely to buy from a store they like the smell of. The scents the company had tested at the time all had colour names. Green Hope, Pink Joy, Blue Kiss, Yellow Wisdom. Sam had thought of how hard it must be to name things, and even harder to distill the essence of a colour.

"Are you okay?" The customer asks her.

"You would look great in a coral polo," Sam says.

Two cake girls come back into the store with salad in a plastic bowl. They stare as though Sam is the wrong kind of person. Her hands shake; her skin breathes in fake ocean; her taste buds crave dark roast.

Jill hands Sam a tissue, steps in to finish the transaction. Sam is relegated to reorganizing the stockroom for the rest of her shift. Sizes organized smallest to largest, boxes of lip gloss and scents moved from one shelf to another. Sam dabs at her wet cheeks with the sleeve of a cardigan and vows to buy it when she gets her next paycheque.

At the end of her shift, Sam waits at the door. Jill stands next to the new manager while he checks the bags of the cake girls, examines their insides with a suspicious eye. Sam holds her leather satchel tight under her arm. Giggling, the cake girls sweep out the door together as one mass of human. The new manager grabs for Sam's bag.

"That woman in the slim fits has been waiting five min-utes at the till," Sam says.

With an elbow, Jill nudges him and huffs. He flits away.

"You'll get used to him."

Jill moves to Sam and again embraces her. Jill smells like sweat from being in that stuffy office working out a schedule all day, hopefully finding enough shifts for Sam to make do. Sam walks out of the store. On the escalator, she reaches into her purse and feels the cold glass bottle, pumps a spray onto her hand. At the top, she cups her hand to her face, covers her eyes and nose and mouth as she passes Starbucks, inhales the stolen ocean.

The Gospel of Kittany

A slender boy with a neat bun emerges from underneath a geometric-printed linen skirt. He kneels at Kittany's feet, keeps his hands to himself now. She sighs and brings her thighs together.

"You did very well today." She wipes his mouth with a soft blue washcloth, holds his face in her hand for a moment, shares a half smile, then points to the door. He exits the gazebo, splits the filmy white gauze with his perfect young body. Wind doesn't whip through this wide swath of land; there's only ever a slight breeze. Mountains hold the valley in a tight circle. The parade of young men in and out of this gazebo, her bedroom, the rose garden, and the milking shed produces a steadier whip of air.

Kittany taps a message on her phone, then takes a selfie and sends it to her Instagram followers. She shares when she's satisfied. In two minutes, she will have hundreds of little hearts beating underneath her image. She uses hashtags sparingly. She doesn't wear makeup. But she gets her followers' attention. She's filled with love and affection.

Kittany. That was her nickname as a child. Her given name, Brittany, just never conveyed how cute she was. Her small feline lips and almond eyes gave her the look of a kitten at the height of its precociousness. Her father would spin her in the front yard, and she would mew and giggle. Her mother would pet her long soft hair. Kittany, Kittany, Kittany.

After she'd started *The Light* online, it took a few months to build steam, to crack through to the people who would take her seriously in the way she wanted to be taken seriously. The site gained traction through her commitment to social media. She'd already had a decent following from her modelling career. She wasn't huge, but some of her most interesting shoots circulated on Tumblr in the right circles. Posing as zookeeper to taxidermy fails, standing in a hall of mirrors for a nude editorial, wearing a ballgown and tiara with a kaleidoscope of butterflies in a cactus field. Modelling had given her a platform, and now she was expanding it. She couldn't sell products anymore; she had to promote something bigger.

Her advisor, Tim, had been a small-time talent agent before she came along. It was easy to wrangle him into helping her with this movement. She was twenty and alluring and didn't take no for an answer. Her voice high but charming. He had always been supportive of her, had taken her modelling career seriously when others had doubted. She'd made money because of their work together.

When she'd appeared at her first casting call in a light denim skirt and a souvenir aquarium T-shirt, Tim barely batted an eye at her. Someone at her school had mentioned there was an open call for teen models. But when they asked her to pull her hair back, put on the plain black crewneck to do test shots, something must have clicked. He approached her father, standing behind a folding chair, compulsively checking his watch, and shook his hand.

"Your daughter has something," he said but didn't elaborate. That's not how these things work. It must be kept vague, up to interpretation.

One of her parents' friends had said that she was tall enough and even attractive enough to be a model, and so she looked into the logistics: age range of models, how much money they made, how quickly they could retire. Realizing her age was optimal, she begged her parents to take her to the model call. Her mother wasn't thrilled, had dropped a jar of salsa on the kitchen floor in shock. This wasn't a serious pursuit, something long-term. They'd negotiated. If she managed to get work, all money saved would be put away for school. It could be a learning experience, a chance to find out more about herself. Her father would drive her, his little girl next to him in the car as they made their way anywhere she needed to go.

That was eight years ago. Since then, Tim and Kittany have travelled the world, become business partners, founded this beautiful movement together. She couldn't tell what he thought of fourteen-year-old Kittany, so committed to doing everything by the book, constantly studying fashion magazines and Jane Austen. But by the time they'd moved into the warehouse space, started organizing *The Light*, he seemed to understand that she meant business.

Early on he'd questioned her name. They were sitting on folding chairs in a meeting circle. It looked like a group therapy session, except they were passing around a fat growler of homemade alcohol, everyone swigging if they had a good idea, something approved by Kittany.

"Brittany, or even Brit, are not what I'm about anymore. I need to leave those names behind. My parents gave me this nickname, and it's going to be who I am. Cats, even kittens, are independent. They have a sexual look."

"What if you use a man's name?" he asked.

She threw the bottle of grain alcohol on the tile floor. Brown shards of glass exploded all around her. Alcohol pooled at her feet, soaking through her slim designer flats.

"What if you shut up like a man?" she'd said and stood up on her chair.

Everyone stopped talking and watched the pools of booze curl around on the concrete. Tim spent that evening mopping and cleansing with lemons and sleeping in a cold grey corner. She couldn't get rid of him. He was smart. And she liked that he wanted to question authority, that he acknowledged her as authority.

Kittany has the Light. This is what she makes clear to her followers. Though she doesn't call them followers. She calls them her Devotees. Because she believes in devotion, because devotion is love. Love comes from lust. Sex is the way to connect with light, hers being the brightest.

Boys line up to please her. They believe they will be touched by something intangible that will make them better. That by pleasuring her they are holding fast to hope. They believe. Kittany is careful not to break the law. So many who came before her made huge mistakes because they believed they were owed everything. Kittany wants to earn her Devotees. To have them follow her, please her, help her create a new world order from scratch. There are codes to follow in society that aren't laws or strict rules but ways of being. Don't break the trust of those who are devoted is her main one.

They've been hidden away for almost a year. Amassing Devotees wasn't difficult. At twenty-two, she's the youngest leader of a new religion in decades. She tweets her devotionals. She's been featured in *Buzzfeed*, *Vice*, *New York Magazine*, and many small online publications. She had a six-page feature in *Vanity Fair*; Annie Lebovitz photographed her. Annie, wearing a satin sleep mask, was transported from the airport in the passenger seat of a Smart car driven by the largest of Kittany's guardians. She was delivered back to the airport the same way, with the radio playing classic rock and her eyes again covered in the sleep mask. She didn't see the large gate that separated the Devotional from the one-lane highway and lush hills.

A large print of the photograph hangs in the attic loft of Kittany's home. She's wearing a long, low-cut black dress, her long honey hair in a messy bun on her head, copper and silver and gold necklaces dangling at different lengths, some punctuated by rough crystals and stones. She'd been listening to a lot of Stevie Nicks, combed through every photo of her ever taken. The backdrop of the photo is the gazebo, the cornerstone of the Devotional. The gauzy curtains are wide open and behind her, the earth tones in the mountains seem to mimic her hazel eyes and not the other way around. That's the magic of Lebovitz in post-production. Kittany gives out small versions of this image, encased in vintage lockets, to the young girls who flock to be a part of what she's doing. They believe. That they can achieve high levels of devotion, carry light in their bodies, too. They dress like her, wear their hair how she's wearing hers, sometimes even mimic her tone of voice.

Tim waves his hand through the curtains and then stomps into the gazebo. He's supposed to make his presence known, not interrupt her, be respectful. No one is supposed to interrupt anyone. Kittany doesn't tolerate general rudeness.

"Thanks for knocking," she says, rubs homemade lavender balm into her dry elbows.

"How is anyone supposed to knock on a fucking curtain?"

"You know what I mean."

He grabs the patchwork pouf from under Kittany's feet and sits down in front of her.

"Well, I've been trying to take things literally," he says, eyes the moisturizer.

Kittany digs deep into the squat Mason jar and pulls out more balm, massages it into her cuticles. Elbows resting on his knees, head resting on his hands balled together, he looks like he's ready to question her about something she doesn't want to be questioned about. She presses her newly moisturized feet through the tent of his arms and rests them on his lap.

"Can I ask you to tell me why you're here right now?" she asks.

"I want to talk to you about your presentation. The way you're presenting your presentations, really. I still feel like something is missing. An elevation of ideas. Or the way you act, as if they're not elevated ideas. You're not giving yourself a high enough power."

She rubs her feet together, presses them against each other, heels close to his crotch.

"Is that the way you talked to the guy you managed from those used car commercials? Wondering if he could present himself better? You were a talent agent. Your job was to trust the talent, convince other people of that talent. Not to completely disregard everything they say and do. There is no higher power, Tim."

Atheism and agnosticism are popular. Growing in numbers. She is a part of this. There is no higher power. There is The Light. There are orgasmic good times. There is love in many forms: some more superficial, some deeper, some platonic, some romantic, and some frivolous but pure, like the love of artisanal salted caramel ice cream. Making a person lovable, herself included, wasn't as easy. She's still working on it. How she appears, every selfie, every Snapchat, every statement she makes. They can't be statements. That's for politicians. She has to remain genuine.

Getting in touch with people who used to casually worship God, or yoga, or home renovation television seemed difficult at first. But, in fact, that was so easy.

When they were an urban organization, it was always open calls for gatherings. Post events on Facebook. Leave artfully designed handbills at Whole Foods. Construct a beautiful setting with paper crafts in a warehouse space. Supply fancy canapés and artisanal drinks in mason jars. People need to believe they'll live lavishly. Trade in pleasure. Then see the importance of frugality too. Get them crafting with recycled materials. Old clothes into a quilt. Restructure a Coach purse into a compost bin. Guilt. That's the foundation of belief.

Sermons are for old men who want to tear people down. She deals in presentations. When she was a child, her mother was the one who convinced their family to stop going to church. They could be good people without it. It was the first time she'd heard the word "patriarchy," though coming out of her mother's mouth she wasn't sure how it related to sitting in pews and group hymn singing. Kittany was disappointed. At church, there were so many people; she could socialize with kids and have adults touch her face and tell her how beautiful she was. Her father always let her get ice cream and pie after church. Her mother said they could still get pie on Sundays. But they never did.

Today she is due to deliver an online presentation. The video accompaniment is ready and after she's done talking, livestreaming everyone the way they live so peacefully, flicking from slides of young men politely handing her slippers and robes in the morning to clips of mountain sheep locking horns to get access to a ewe, gain possession of a woman because they are animals, not humans, the whole thing will be available for $2.99 on iTunes.

"Kittany, I know there's no higher power."

"We're still building this, and I have the attention of a lot of people. Time. That's what we need. How many Twitter followers will it take to get you to stop harassing me?"

"Kardashian numbers, Kit. That's ideal."

The heel of her foot bumps his package with intent to harm. He whimpers and covers himself. Kittany ignores it, composes a tweet:

@GospelofKittany Sometimes we just need to send love. Let's devote ourselves to love. We are all in this together. #loveotional

Tim's phone buzzes in his pants pocket. He gets updates whenever Kittany tweets, posts on Facebook. Whenever she does anything. An instant Google alert to remind him that she's the one making things happen.

He even gets the bad news, the negative reviews, as he calls them. Even though she doesn't believe what they do can be reviewed like a blockbuster. It's not the same type of output, creation. This is something organic.

Young people have been positive, loving her posts, sending her private messages, crying over how she's transformed their lives, smiling and confessing how much they love her, making homemade shirts with her face on them, holding up signs that quote her messages of love. But older people have tried to take her down with words. A few articles crop up every so often, and she does her best to listen, read, absorb but not let it affect her. The work, her love, is what matters, what must be cultivated. If a columnist for the *Globe and Mail* thinks she's vapid, then they aren't looking hard enough. At the work she's really doing. At the response. At themselves.

She doesn't think she has all the answers. Sometimes it's okay to be criticized. "Consider critics. How else will we know that we're doing something wrong, how else do we consider how to be better?" She'd tweeted with a #betterlives. It got 10K retweets and responses from across North America, some from across the world. People who felt changed, who told stories in 140 characters of becoming more aware of the world around them, cooking for the homeless, volunteering to build houses for strangers in another country, recycling their beer cans for the first time in their lives.

Not every tweet is equal. A few months ago, she posted a selfie posed in the rushing creek with her hair cascading over one eye, the rushing water further brightening her luminous skin. The caption read "It's okay to feel free."

This triggered an onslaught of reactions.

"Kittany is coy."

"Kittany is too beautiful."

"Kittany is sexist."

"Kittany acts like it's so easy to just do whatever you feel like."

"Kittany is smug."

"Kittany doesn't understand what life truly means."

"Kittany is blasphemous."

"Kittany only worships Kittany."

Tim and her team had analyzed the responses, yet couldn't quite figure out what had caused the reaction. The image, the words, her wet skin, her hair, a squirrel on the grassy bank in the corner of the frame, a combination of everything? She keeps these negative quotes about herself. She saves them, as the tweets and comments scroll on a screen above her kneeling desk. Apparently, Beyoncé does something similar. Kittany admires her, wishes she was better at dancing. It brings people together.

Presentation 22: Seeds of Change

Open on a sweeping shot of the Devotional. Mountains and trees, vibrant and glowing. Young men, shirtless, pick fruit from trees with shimmering leaves.

Voice-over: *Mountains and trees are the perfect shade of green. We don't try to improve on nature's spectrum. But we are imperfect. And yet, that is what makes us perfect. That is what makes us able to understand our need for more, our need to change, our need to grow. And, yes, sometimes our failure. But we are together.*

Kittany: Hello, I'm Kittany, founder of *The Light*, here at the Devotional. Every time we make a move in our lives, things change. Even when we think things stay the same, that our routines are locked in, that we've figured out the best way to live our lives, there are moments of adjustment. A broken water heater that prevents us from cleaning the dishes, which prevents us from cleaning our home, which prevents us from feeling clean.

Change happens, even when we try to ward it off in every way. We become anxious. And why wouldn't we? The world does not want us to be as one. The world does not want us to indulge in simple pleasures. It wants to drive us apart.

Cut to the Boy, pacing in front of the gazebo. He's barefoot, and his curly hair makes him look like a poodle puppy. There's worry in his eyes, as if someone's forgotten him at a gas station.

Voice-over: *Even the young and beautiful experience anxiety. How can we make a change for those in our lives, those who seem to have things we wish we had? How can we put love ahead of jealousy? Really see other people with our eyes and the eyes that burst from within us, from somewhere we can't accurately define: the irises of the soul. We can never know the burdens of others, unless we communicate and show love.*

Cut to Kittany approaching the Boy with artisanal toast and fresh jam. She hands him the toile-printed plate, then holds out her arms. He sets down the plate and bombards her. In her arms he's burrowed deep.

Close up: The Boy inhaling Kittany's chest, deep breaths in. She strokes his bare arm.

Kittany: Small things can become big gestures. Each small step to affection might seem insignificant. But that's because of our perception. See each little moment, each slice of toast, smear of jam. We make those things with our hands, and then we use our hands to embrace each other. Touch someone today. Observe the change. And write to us here. We love hearing your stories. We see you. Sending Love and Devotion.

A text graphic starts small, zooms forward until it fills the screen: Try Change xoxo

"Thank you. You did so well today. I know you haven't been involved in many presentations." Kittany pets the Boy's curls.

"Thank you, ma'am." He stands over her, taller by at least half a foot.

"Don't call me ma'am. I'm not old enough for that." He's only eighteen, and she doesn't feel like a ma'am, though she's careful to never call herself a girl.

"Sorry."

"Don't apologize."

"Okay."

They stand in front of the gazebo as the camerawomen and crew move the cameras, booms, and mics. The women all smile at her, and she gives them reassuring looks. They'll need to edit everything together for the iTunes release. Kittany's proud of them. Efficient and skilled, they always make sure the music, the graphics, every detail is on message. The artistry of these videos can't tread into the realm of cheese.

"Great one today, Kit," Marian says, pats her on the back and struts with her camera bag on her shoulder.

"I think we should do some more long shots next time," Greta says.

Kittany nods her head. Thinks about visual impact.

"Thank you for continuing to do such good voice-over work, Emma. I know they'll re-record you, but it really helps for me to hear the words as we move and interact."

While she's talking to Emma, the Boy turns to her as if he

has something to say. Before the Boy can talk, Tim barges between them, grips Kittany's shoulder. "Kit. Did you get that toast recipe from *goop* last week?"

She's talked to too many men today, even though she's surrounded herself with women. Somehow there are still always so many men talking. Kittany ignores Tim, walks hand in hand with the Boy to the wellness centre. They need to recharge with massages and triangles of avocado. The Boy will be silent, in awe of her. He won't obstruct her devotion.

After reviewing articles and books and news reports, Kittany knew that total control wasn't her game. All those men writing their manifestos and enforcing them with an iron fist only made them more vulnerable to people wanting to take them down. L. Ron Hubbard, David Koresh, Jim Jones. They were wanted men, not because of their bad ideas but because of what they did. Because of their abuse, how they didn't respect people. Every one of them used their people like stepstools. While trying to convince their followers of their undeniable brilliance, were they not also thinking of them as underlings at the same time? If people don't want to be invested in what she's creating, they can leave. Devotion can't come from control. Love doesn't live in abuse.

Before the Devotional was a real place, she'd gone to visit her mother. She was proud of Kittany for giving up modelling, proud, too, of how she'd managed herself in that world—she'd made money; she wasn't holed up in a hotel room with rock stars and opiates. In the kitchen, Kittany and her mother were canning all the excess vegetables from the garden. Her father had gone on the first of many trips to his parents, who were both suffering with bad backs. Without Kittany and her father around to eat, the fresh vegetables were going to go rotten.

"I see you're still wearing those crystals. We used to love crystals in the seventies, too. I should get some of my old ones out for you."

"It's not about fashion, Mom."

"Oh, I know, Kit."

"It's about a lot more."

"Well, I still don't understand what it is you're doing now. Are you a party planner?"

Her mother is chopping the stems off beets while Kittany stands at the sink rinsing green beans. Right after Kittany started modelling, her mother had gone through a brief weight-loss kick. The dark wooden cupboards filled with pre-packaged bars and shakes. Unlike the way their kitchen was usually stocked, a mix of fresh vegetables, hearty breads, and cookies and candies were stashed in an old tin in the pantry. It didn't last long. Her mother couldn't handle the way the other women talked about themselves at meetings, how expensive and tasteless the boxed food was.

"Mom, this project I'm working on. It's something really big."

Kittany abandoned her green bean post and rushed to the hallway, came back with a stack of papers. Her mother held up her purpled hands as Kittany showed her the design for the Devotional, the first draft of her first presentation, photos of her standing in the empty field where it will all happen. She recited a message of love. Her mother's face dropped.

"Is this what you want to do with your life? How you'll spend all that money you just made? It's absurd."

Kittany grabs the papers, holds them to her chest. She stands and opens her mouth but doesn't speak. As she turns to leave, her mother reaches out, tries to catch her arm. Instead, she wipes a beet stain all over Kittany's $195 T-shirt, leaves a smear on the papers in her arms. Their last communication.

Her mother didn't want to understand her, or her goals. She didn't even want to try. This is why Kittany hasn't spoken to her in two years. Her father had long been too embarrassed about how much she'd bared as a model. The reason her parents are now separated is because of her career. Her father couldn't handle what he'd helped Kittany to achieve, and her mother couldn't invest in his absurd moaning about it. Her father's moved back to his small hometown across the country, to be near his aging parents. That day, Kittany left her mother alone in the only place she'd considered home. She didn't have to explain why she needed to make a new place for herself.

The people at the Devotional have jobs, work to do. But every minute of their lives isn't scheduled. It's Canada in the twenty-first century, and they have cable and craft beer and whatever else they need to unwind. People are filming crimes on their iPhones and documenting cats shoving a variety of objects off tables. It's so easy to get in trouble if you demand every ounce of every person. It's so easy to get into trouble. Images can cause problems.

At night there are organized events: beer tastings, knitting circles, movie nights, games nights. The first few weeks there were so few of them, and every night they gathered around a campfire, drank spirits, told stories, listened to her personal playlist on an iPhone in a tin cup. As more joined, it seemed necessary to organize. But it's not a home for the elderly. No one enforces participation. You don't have to make a turkey out of a tracing of your hand.

She remembers modelling. Every hour taken up by something she didn't feel devoted to. Everyone whose salary she paid cared about how she looked, what she ate, the kind of salads she posted pics of online. When she was alone, she slept or stayed awake thinking about how everyone in her life was thinking about her. Being alone didn't mean relaxing or enjoying herself. Some nights she'd lay awake, images of term papers and science experiments floating behind her closed eyes. Missing schoolwork and basic kid drudgery. That seemed like recreation.

As soon as she'd gotten a little bit of online attention, even fifteen hundred Instagram followers, her presence felt huge to her. Bigger than she'd dreamed. Because at that time, she hadn't dreamed at all. She was still a high school student, shuffling around to casting calls and photo shoots, and there they were, double tapping little hearts under photos of her in underwear sewn by children just a few years younger than she was.

In bed, Kittany tweets and retweets. So many young people are sending her their stories, their feelings, are revealing themselves in words and photos and emojis. A young woman in Alberta always believed she could never come out to her family. A boy from Nova Scotia who'd suffered horrible burns shared photos of his body, even though he was so ashamed of his skin that he hadn't looked at himself in the mirror in over two years.

And now, older people her parents' age, they too are sharing. There are a few out there who are able to understand devotion. Reclaiming their lives, understanding the value of things they'd never considered: women breaking free of loveless marriages, retired couples taking selfies together, the transformative power of memes. Lately these are her bedtime stories. She hates to admit to herself that usually these warm her heart more than the stories from people closer to her age.

One woman has been emailing her once a week. She caught the eye of the team filtering her emails because she is from Kittany's hometown.

The tone was sharp and sweet. The first had been a simple message of praise.

"This is good work you're doing."

This woman is anonymous. Not concerned with being seen. No avatar. Sometimes she gives criticism.

"When you say that love comes from lust, are you really thinking about what love means? It feels callous."

Sometimes concern.

"You might want to consider taking a break. Just a day for yourself."

It is hard not to see her mother in this woman. It is hard not to think about her mother sometimes. It is hard not to reach out.

"Can I talk to you?"

Emma's booming voice breaks through the silence of the night. Kittany pats the left side of the bed, and Emma sits beside her.

"I know you don't like gossip, but this is something I need you to hear. I didn't mean to." Emma stops and nervously gropes at the dangling tassels on the cotton drapes.

Kittany gets up from her bed and walks to the bar in the far corner of the tent. She knows Emma wouldn't interrupt if it wasn't something actually important or something that would burden her or others to keep to herself. She's also talks to Kittany like she's a real person, not some magical entity.

"I heard him talking. I was walking by, and I didn't mean to, but he was so loud. Yelling. And then it sounded like he was, I don't know, pushing someone, and then something fell over, and then I came here."

"Can you tell me what he said?"

Kittany hands Emma a glass, and she nods to pour the whisky. They both take a drink.

"It was hard to hear for sure, but it was something like 'I

want to make sure we've got her while she's still viable. Women, they don't age like men do. We have time. There's time. But how much time?' Something like that. Shit, I'm so sorry."

She'd heard him say things like this before. Back in her modelling days. "Most men remain virile and sexually alluring for years. Well into their sixties." "Women need to put in more effort." And "Bodies have a clock all right, on when their ability to make money expires." As a teenager, she'd just put on her headphones and become absorbed in sounds that weren't his voice. Not because of the content but because he was always talking so much, and like any teenager, she got tired of adults shouting on high about anything and everything they felt. Maybe they didn't know better.

Her skin, her face, her body, it's all going to fall, change. The value system Tim trades in will leave her behind. Kittany radiates with rage. This is rudeness. She's given him so much of her. Allowed him to represent her ideas, her ideals.

"Can you stay for a while? Can we talk about something else?"

"Sure," Emma says, and they sit together, pass the bottle back and forth.

"Did you read *Eat Pray Love*?"

"Part of it," Emma says. "I got half way through pray and then I fell asleep on a Greyhound bus and left it on the seat when I got off. I didn't get to the love part."

"It was over-rated. Not sexy enough. I listened to the audiobook, though."

"Nothing is ever sexy enough for you."

Kittany chokes on her swig of whisky.

"Do you really think that's true?"

Emma yawns. Kittany knows she was up early today on an errand to a farm, sourcing some goats for the Devotional. Baby goats will look adorable in photographs, and everyone is already excited to make and share cute baby goat videos.

"Real answer? Sort of. You like to push things. Sometimes further than others would. Not in an offensive way, though."

Emma yawns again, body fading. Her wrist tips to the side, and the last bit of her drink almost drains onto the bed. Kittany takes the glass and sets it on the nightstand. She cradles Emma and strokes her hair. The night is so quiet. Sometimes it startles Kittany still, no street noise, vehicles, people shouting to themselves. A coyote howl doesn't count as night noise. Emma slumps into sleep, her dark hair spread across Kittany's lap and onto the creamy pillows.

Presentation 23: Physical Devotion

Kittany sits in the Wellness Centre lobby eating fresh, fat strawberries.

Voice-over: *Love. This is what we believe in. Each other. The flowing wave of feeling that overcomes us when we are able to connect as one. Sometimes we can love a small act. The simple joy of tasting the sweet flesh of a strawberry. But sometimes we need a more intimate connection.*

Through these acts of sexual touching, we come to love. First we engage with consent; we look at each other; we nod our heads or say we want to proceed. Proceed to experience Devotional transformation. And in the end, we change through sex, through fucking or making love.

Cut to the Boy. Kittany removes her custom-embroidered silk robe. Underneath she's wearing a slim floral cotton bandeau. The Boy rushes to her side. He pulls the bandeau up over her breasts. He kisses them. She nods. He presses his face between them, brings his hands to each, and touches them until she tells him to remove the bandeau.

The camera is too far away to see her tongue, but it can focus in on her face, head thrown back, not looking to see who is judging, who is worried, who cares what she looks like while she is trying to make her body feel better, to make the world a better place. Behind them, the sun is cresting over the mountain, a rosy slip of sky.

Voice-over: *The body has secrets, but the body is also a storyteller. Those secrets can be revealed to another person through body language, through gestures, and through our sensual connections.*

"You know why this is bad?" Tim is furious. He stalks onto the simple set like a caricature of an angry Hollywood mogul.

Kittany wanted the scene filmed in the morning. Not just for the morning light, those golden hues that create a warm glow, but also because she wasn't in the mood to be combative. Tim is a night owl and usually sleeps in. Kittany high-fives Greta and gives Emma a hug, a long hug.

"I know why you think it's bad, but it's on brand. Not everything is about what you think."

"On brand? A slutty, immature brand! You're fucked," Tim shouts through his grogginess.

She calls out to her number one performer and stalks away, Tim stumbling after her with his morning coffee in a metal camp mug. The Boy runs ahead to catch Kittany, her hand outstretched to him.

#sensualconnections starts trending. Kittany enlists a group at the Devotional to Instagram themselves in whatever poses feel beautiful to them. She selects only those who are engaged and excited about baring their bodies, about entwining their limbs. They make eleven-second make-out videos. Encourage their devoted to do the same. Young people everywhere slipping tongues into each other's mouths, showing skin, baring parts of their bodies in slips and flashes and filters. Their stories fill 140 characters, detail sensual experiences, fumbling first encounters and masturbation fails, their never-ending virginity. Young women sexualized by older men. Boys unsure of how not to offend girls.

It's like this for a while. Honest and loving. Kittany, alone at night, taking time to look and read. She catches the glimmers of fear in their eyes when they pose, the vulnerable curls of their lips as they kiss, the delicate trails of saliva, the stretch marks and appendix scars, the acne, the makeup applied without the help of professionals. They'd all look gorgeous in a magazine. A special publication for the devoted. Her people seeing her people in glossy print.

Free Wi-Fi was to allow those living in the Devotional to express themselves, to communicate easily. The IT team was great at fixing any issues, and not once did Kittany think to snoop, to set up surveillance on phones and laptops.

But right under her nose, Tim pulled out his phone and contacted everyone he could think of who would be looking for a scoop, a hot tip. He didn't need to hide. In the middle of the night, while she lay in bed, propped on pillows, scrolling, dabbing feeds with emojis, he got in touch with all his old contacts. He told them that she was almost always naked and made everyone compliment her constantly, that she had to look in a mirror for an hour every day, that she forced people to touch her sexually, that she forced herself on people, that she was abusive. The rumours didn't need to be true. The spin cut her, everyone waiting to go negative.

Major news outlets reported that she was a sex addict, that the boy was underaged, that she was flying too close to the sun. Entertainment television reported that she was paying those living at the Devotional for sex. Religious groups protested her hold on youth, alleged that teen pregnancy was spiking, that chlamydia was making a comeback with eighteen to twenty-five- year-olds. And all of it was her fault. She was ruining society, a poison to the youth of today.

"Would anyone care if she wasn't young and photogenic?" asks one talking head.

"There's no doubt she thinks she can get away with anything. She's used to getting away with everything because she's beautiful," responds another.

"Exactly. Kids listen to what comes out of her mouth because she might as well be a pop star, mindlessly singing the word 'baby' over and over again." The talking head pounds the desk for emphasis.

"I give her religious movement another six months. If she doesn't Heaven's Gate them all—coerce them into a glamorous mass suicide. Gorgeous bodies, dead in designer sneakers."

On the night of her nineteenth birthday, Tim had taken her phone right out of her hand and shot so many photos of her in an exclusive booth at a cocktail lounge. Sipping from expensive drinks, as she has on so many other nights, she's surrounded in the dim light by other models. Together they crowd around the booth, all dressed to make the world jealous of their ease at being alive.

"Put these online," he'd instructed her.

Tim knew it was the right moment. She was transitioning from a child model that people wanted to know, be near to, touch, to an adult model that people wanted to know, be near to, touch. The next morning, as she looked at the confetti stickers and hearts and stars decorating her posts, she realized how calculating Tim was, how he knew his business. She could legally drink, a new stage in her career that had been so carefully constructed. It was serious business.

And this was no different. To him, spreading lies was the right way to go. A counterpoint to her presentation. Balance in the universe. A challenge for her to overcome. He did it all from a hundred yards away while she wrote notes to herself, while she thought about the lives of these young people growing up, hating themselves. And then he stole an ATV and slipped away, the phone she'd paid for zipped safely into his waterproof jacket pocket.

Kittany pulls up her old photo shoots, compares her poses then and now. Her arm draped over her head in the underwear ad is identical to her arm in a recent post about letting go of anger. A coy look on her face in a black and white shot from her first year as a model pairs perfectly with last year's "Love Yourself" meme series. This is no different. How many times have her devotees described her as beautiful, commented on her presentation outfits, screamed in Snapchat their jealousy of her glossy hair. Her face still the reason she coerces people.

Kittany emails the anonymous woman. She wants to check in with her; it's her first instinct. But she hasn't received a response. And Kittany is constantly checking to make sure.

In seclusion, the news playing on her iPhone, she scrolls and scrolls. For the first time since all of this happened, she cried. She covered her body in thin blankets, even though it was the heat of summer. Like when she was first modelling on those long days, she couldn't stand her body anymore. It was part of her but also not, like she could rip it from herself, and then lightly slip out of it and float away.

After a night of ignoring anyone who came to her bedroom, a night alone shouting, sobbing, running every mistake and failure in her mind, she posts a video. A close-up of her face. Smears of mascara. Red-streaked eyes. A sniffle of snot threatening to emerge from a nostril. In the allotted seconds, she expresses the importance of intimacy, of consent. How every expression of ourselves we might normally be afraid of is actually beautiful.

"Everyone. All ages. Women, especially, if you think you've aged out of beauty: ignore. You're sexy and magical. Share with me. I'm opening my direct messages. I want to see you. I am not the only face."

Then she uses her finger to scribble over her own face, like black Sharpie straight over the screen.

And they do send her photos. Flooded with grainy selfies, black-and-white butts, wrinkled cleavage. These women are her, and she will be them. Their revealing captions, their stories, their images. People need to see these. Does it matter if she loses followers? They'll come back when they look in the mirror in forty years, when they realize how their eyes and hearts have betrayed them.

One woman sends nudes, six-second sex tapes, a story revealed in body parts. She's sixty-eight. Her son bought her a selfie stick for a trip to Belgium, but instead she's at home in the same bedroom she's had since the day she got married. Above her bare shoulder, a dresser with a wooden jewellery box and family photos. In a shot of her upper body while lying on her bed, Kittany can see a cheap painting of a sunset. The video reveals two older bodies moving together, a pair of department store underwear rolled down a thigh.

Overwhelmed, Kittany can't stop staring at each photo, watches the tiny videos over and over. If only these women were here. They should be here.

Kittany thinks of her mother. Across the country, sitting in her kitchen nook in the early morning dark, drinking coffee. Before she pats on powder, lines around her mouth rising and falling as she chews granola, as she glows in the light of the local morning show. Her mother's body changed from when Kittany first remembers her, from a figure eight to a Weight Watchers casualty twig to a soft strength. She changed her mother's body just by living inside it. Genetics.

Her anonymous woman doesn't send a photo, remains visually inaccessible. But she does send a message. "How are you feeling?"

Kittany imagines Tim holed up in a hotel room with cheap scotch and Bugles, ready to sell a new lie to the press. Reporting her new "obsession" with older women and an unhealthy fixation on aging. Photoshopped images of her with horribly faked, horrible plastic surgery. She never claimed to be psychic, but if Tim doesn't go this route she'll be surprised and a little disappointed. Kittany knows him so well.

Her phone buzzes again, but it's not a notification. It's the Boy. She lets him in. They lay on their stomachs on top of the sheets, scrolling through photos.

"Look at these women," Kittany says.

"Okay."

"Really look."

The Boy scrunches up his aquiline nose.

"See them," she says.

You're so beautiful, everyone always said. *You should be a model.* Kittany knows she should do a lot of things. She should keep trying. Admit her failure. Admire. She should cut off Tim's phone, his paycheque. She should ask these women how she can make them a part of her movement. She hands the phone to the boy and lets him explore, on his own, the bodies.

Kittany lies on her back and looks up at the tent ceiling. By winter, the yurts will be ready. Solid structures erected to protect them from cold and snow. In the lantern light, the creases in the canvas look like a crooked smile. She closes her eyes. Touches the smooth sides of her mouth. Kittany scrolls through an imaginary timeline of her body, her face. By the time she's her mother's age, she'll have documented most of her life. It will be beautiful.

Acknowledgments

Thanks to Kathryn Mockler at *Joyland* and the Writers' Trust of Canada for giving time and space to stories from this collection.

I want to send heartfelt thanks (and refreshments) to Kellee Ngan, Shay Wilson, and Meghan Waitt for looking at earlier drafts of these stories and who are always there to give the best notes and hugs.

To my creative companion for life, Daniel Zomparelli, I give all the thanks. You pushed me, commiserated with me, and drank with me. Without you I couldn't have completed this book.

Thanks to the Lying Bastards, who have seen the roughest of my work over the past twelve years and helped me see these stories through. Sally Breen, Keri Korteling, Nancy Lee, Judy McFarlane, Denise Ryan, Carol Shaben, and John Vigna are all gems as writers and humans.

So much gratitude to Jen Sookfong Lee, Nancy Lee, Anakana Schofield, and Gabe Liedman for your generous words about my words. Thanks to my editor Robyn So, who understood what

I was trying to do. And huge thanks to the delights at Arsenal Pulp Press: Brian, Robert, Susan, Oliver, and of course, Cynara, who is a pal and a confidante, and a totally stellar publicist.

Love and gratitude to Roxan Marucot and Jason Bay who've lived with (and near) me and fed me and have been in my life as long as the oldest stories in this book. And special love to Jag Dost who always checks in on me at the right time.

Thanks as always to my family for their love and support, especially my mom and dad who always thought short stories were cool.

To my nieces, far in the future, I hope you're both as fierce and tender as the women in this book.

Dina Del Bucchia is the author of three collections of poetry: *Coping with Emotions and Otters* (Talonbooks, 2013), *Blind Items* (Insomniac Press, 2014), and *Rom Com* (Talonbooks, 2015), the latter written with her *Can't Lit* podcast co-host Daniel Zomparelli. Her short story, "Under the 'I'," was a finalist for the Writers' Trust RBC Bronwen Wallace Award in 2012. Her work has also appeared in such places as *Event*, *Matrix*, *The Fiddlehead*, *SAD Mag* and *Joyland*, and as art at Old Friends' exhibition Funny Business (Gallery Atsui) and at That One Thing You Said: an exhibit of visual poetry at Verses Festival of Words. She is an editor of *Poetry is Dead* magazine and is the Artistic Director of the Real Vancouver Writers' Series. She lives in Vancouver. *dinadelbucchia.com*

Don't
Tell Me
What to
Do